MW00811119

FIRST COMES DEATH
THEN COMES MARRIAGE
(BOOK 13)

A HARLEY AND DAVIDSON MYSTERY

LILIANA HART

LOUIS SCOTT

DEDICATION

To Bacon (our French Bulldog) & Biscuit (our micro-mini GoldenDoodle)—

You're the best writing partners we could ever ask for, and we're so glad you're standing in for the children as they start to go off to college. It's not weird at all to push dogs around in a baby stroller, no matter what people tell you.

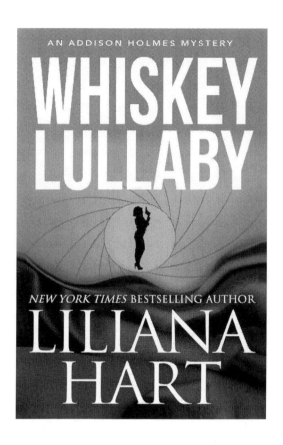

From Liliana's NYT and USA Today bestselling Addison
Holmes Mystery Series, comes Whiskey Lullaby.
Order Your's Today

CHAPTER ONE

Saturday

The drive back to Rusty Gun was mostly quiet, except for Heather singing a slightly off-tune rendition of "Ring of Fire." At lease she wasn't talking. Agatha didn't think her brain was up to the task of following Heather Cartwright's train of thought.

"Do you want me to take you home?" Heather asked. "Those bags under your eyes could hold a milk jug."

"No," Agatha said. "I'm not tired. Or maybe I'm over-tired. All I know is I can't sleep, and I don't want to sit at home by myself remembering what happened."

"Leave it to me, girl. I've got just the thing. We had to miss our spa day at Gloria's yesterday, but I bet if I ask real nice and pay her double she'll get us in lickety-split. Besides, she needs the money. She's a single mom, and her side jobs aren't real reliable. I guess now that the funeral home is shut down, she'll have to go back to waiting tables."

"The funeral home?"

"She did hair and makeup for all the dead people," Heather said. "She's real talented. I hardly recognized Mr.

Oglesby when I saw him last month. He never looked that good when he was living."

Heather pulled into the parking lot of Gloria's Day Spa, but there was only one other car in the lot. The open sign flashed in the window.

"Not much business," Agatha said.

"She's been trying to hire more stylists and technicians," Heather said. "It's real nice on the inside. As nice as any of the spas I've been to in the city. But she works strictly on appointments, and people in Rusty Gun are more of the walk-in crowd. It's a real shame. I don't know what it's going to take to start getting some quality in this town. Come on."

They got out of the car and Agatha felt like she was sucking in the air from a hair dryer. Her clothes stuck to her skin, and she rushed to the door of the salon and pushed it open, the cold air blasting her in the face.

"Good grief," Heather said. "It's hotter than satan's house cat out here." She shut the door behind them and called out, "Gloria, your favorite client is here. And I need the works."

"I don't think she's here," Agatha said, looking around the empty salon. Heather was right, it was as nice as any she'd seen. Very high quality, and the water feature behind the front desk was mesmerizing.

"Gloria?" Heather asked again. "You with a client, honey?"

Agatha walked down a hallway of treatment rooms, but all the doors were open and they were empty inside. The last door on the left was an office, and it was the only one where the door was half open.

Agatha pushed it the rest of the way, but it caught on something. She pushed harder and a bloody hand flopped out onto the carpet. She pushed the door open a little wider and looked into the blank stare of a woman whose face was so swollen and disfigured she wasn't a hundred percent sure it *was* a woman.

Agatha had been through so much over the past couple of days, it barely even registered what she was looking at.

"Heather," Agatha said. "I don't think Gloria is available today."

Heather looked over her shoulder and down at the body on the floor, and then she screamed so loud Agatha was afraid she had permanent hearing damage.

"That's...that's Gloria," Heather said.

"How can you tell?" Agatha asked. "Her face is pretty busted up."

"That's her," Heather insisted. "I recognize the tattoo on the inside of her wrist. It's a lily because that's her daughter's name."

And then the color drained out of Heather's face and her eyes rolled up into her head. Agatha barely caught her in time to pull her out of the way so she didn't land on Gloria's head.

She left Heather on the floor and reached in her purse for her phone, catching a glimpse of herself in the mirror at the end of the hall. She was as pale as Heather, and her hair looked like she'd brushed it with an eggbeater.

"Coil here," Coil said on the other end of the line.

"It's Agatha," she said. "There's been a murder."

"In addition to the murders we're already working?" he asked cautiously.

"They might be related," she said. "Heather and I are at Gloria's Day Spa, and let's just say Gloria is going to need some serious makeup work to make her presentable enough for an open casket. Heather told me Gloria was working for Brad over at the funeral home doing hair and makeup."

"Ahh," Coil said. "I can see how you'd think her murder is related to Brad's. I'm on the way. Have you checked to make sure the killer left? Are you alone?"

Agatha's mouth dropped open. She normally would've thought of that, but her brain was so muddled from exhaustion it slipped her mind.

"Come quick," she told Coil and hung up.

She hadn't heard any sounds coming from any of the rooms, but she took her gun from her handbag just in case. She went back down the hallway to check each of the rooms again. They were still empty, so she moved into the open salon area, but there were no signs anyone had been there recently.

She locked the front door and turned off the open sign, and then she heard Heather groan from the end of the hall, and hurried back to her friend.

Heather's eyes fluttered open, and her pupils were so dilated only a thin edge of blue showed. There was no color in her cheeks and her over-plumped lips were wet with drool.

"Agatha?" Heather called out.

"I'm here," she said. "Just stay where you are."

"What happened? Why am I on the ground? Something doesn't smell so good. I hope it's not me. Did I have too much to drink?"

"You passed out," Agatha told her.

"I told you it was too hot," Heather said. "I don't know how anyone makes it through a Texas summer without dying of heatstroke. I should file a complaint."

"Unless you're filing it with God's HR department, I think you're just going to have to live with the heat," Agatha said.

Heather rolled to her side and came face to face with

Gloria Chimes. Agatha winced as the color leeched out of Heather's face again.

"I told you to stay down," Agatha said.

"I think I'm going to barf," Heather said, swallowing.

"Not on the crime scene," Agatha said, pulling Heather back by her halter top and moving them down the hallway. She knew it was only a matter of time before the shock wore off and Heather lost her mind.

Three, two, one...

Heather screamed again, and this time the scream was accompanied by unintelligible sobs. "Why does this always happen to me? Why?" she screeched. "I'm tired of finding bodies. There's dead bodies all over the place. I think it's because of you. You're a dead body magnet."

"Calm down," Agatha said. "Coil is on the way."

Even as she tried to reassure Heather, there was banging on the front door and Coil called out, "It's me. Open the door."

Her legs wobbled as she got to her feet and she leaned against the wall to catch her balance. She was lightheaded, and she hoped she didn't embarrass herself by passing out. She was just overtired. That's all it was.

"Get it together, Agatha," she said to herself.

By the time she got to the glass door, Coil looked like he was about ready to bust it in. She hurried and unlocked it, and he pushed his way in with an *oomph* as the cold air hit him.

"You okay?" he asked.

"Yeah, we're just shaken up a bit," she said. "Heather's sitting in the hallway."

"Where's the body?"

"In the office at the end of the hall on the left."

"You look like you're about to drop," Coil said. "Have a

seat on that couch and I'll bring Heather to you. I'm going to call in the team."

Agatha didn't have to be told twice. She took a seat on the black leather couch in the waiting area, and Heather came out to join her a couple of minutes later.

Heather had already texted Karl to come pick her up and take her home. Agatha was pretty sure Coil would want Karl working the scene, but nobody told Heather no when she got something in her head.

They didn't have to wait long for Deputy Karl Johnson and Sergeant Joe Springer to come through the door. They'd already cordoned off the parking lot and set up the perimeter, and Lieutenant Rodriguez was on duty outside to make sure reporters or the curious stayed back where they were supposed to.

"Trouble seems to be following you around," Karl said to Agatha.

He leaned down to kiss Heather, and she wrapped her arms around his neck and buried her face in his shoulder. "Let's go home. I need a drink and a nap."

"Just give me a few minutes, sugar," Karl said. "I need to ask you a few questions and talk to the sheriff for a bit."

It didn't take long for Karl to take their statements. They'd not seen any suspicious cars or people hanging around, and they'd only been inside a couple of minutes before they'd found the body. Agatha recalled everything she could about what had happened, but Heather was no help whatsoever. She had to be the most unobservant person on the face of the planet. Unless someone was committing a fashion faux pas. Then she noticed.

"I know this is because of Brad," Agatha said. "It's because of him that those mercenaries came to town in the first place. Hank's sisters managed to kill one of them, and

Hank and I finished off the others, but they told us someone was coming to extract them. That means there's another who's close by. If Gloria overheard something at the funeral home she wasn't supposed to she'd be considered a loose end."

Coil had come back into the lobby in time to hear what she'd said. "I'm not so sure," he said. "Whoever did this was in a rage. It was personal. Her face and body were beaten so badly she's barely recognizable."

"Is that cause of death?" Agatha asked.

"I don't know," Coil said. "It could be the scissors sticking out of her chest. Or maybe that was just overkill. We'll need to wait for the medical examiner to make a final ruling on cause of death. What I'd like to know is how long she's been here. This looks like a fresh kill. You two are lucky you didn't run into the killer."

"Yeah, I'm full of luck lately," Agatha said, trying to smile.

"Did you or Heather go into the office?" he asked.

"No, I didn't want to contaminate anything, and I wanted to clear Heather out before she barfed all over your crime scene."

"Thoughtful of you," Coil said, making Karl chuckle. "There's blood everywhere. I'm going to have to suit up before I can go all the way inside. Let me know when Deputy James gets here. I need pictures ASAP."

Coil caught himself, and an odd contortion of grief and embarrassment etched itself across his face. James's death was still so fresh neither could imagine the reality that he wouldn't be walking through the door any minute.

"I'm sorry," Coil said, clearing his throat.

Agatha put her hand on his shoulder and squeezed. "No need to apologize."

He nodded and went out to his truck to get booties and a disposable suit. If there was as much blood as he said there was it was going to be a mess to wade through to process the scene.

Coil was only gone a few minutes, and he brought Springer a suit and booties too. Springer sighed, but put them on stoically, and then they went back down the hall where the body was.

Agatha stepped outside for a moment to warm up. She was chilled through, and her teeth were starting to chatter as the reality of what had happened set in. She breathed in the hot air, and tears pooled in her eyes and trailed down her cheeks. She couldn't seem to help it.

This was all her fault. If she'd waited for a team to go in and catch the mercenaries instead of her going on a search for the hearse by herself, maybe Hank wouldn't be stuck in the hospital, and Gloria would still be alive. Their wedding would happen right on schedule, and they'd both be well enough to enjoy a much-needed honeymoon.

She couldn't help but cry a little harder. Everything was ruined, and people were still dying.

"None of this is your fault, you know," Karl said.

She hadn't realized he'd followed her outside.

"You didn't throw Hank off that ledge and mess up his back," he continued. "You tried calling for backup, and no one answered your call. Sometimes that happens. But your gut told you time was of the essence and you went for it. We'll eventually put all the pieces of this mess together, and everything will go back to normal."

She chewed on her lip. She wanted to yell and scream at him. How did he know everything was going back to normal? Hank was paralyzed for Pete's sake. He was going to be wheelchair bound for the foreseeable future. Things might never be normal again.

"Come on back inside," Karl said. "The media is here."

They walked back into the air-conditioned salon, and goose bumps pebbled on her bare arms.

Coil came out once the medical examiner arrived to make room in the office, and he came back into the lobby, his suit and booties smeared with blood.

"These mercenaries were all armed," Coil said. "They shot at Hank's sister. Brad was killed with multiple gunshot wounds. And guns were their weapons of choice when they tried to run you and Hank down at the meatpacking plant."

"What are you saying?" Agatha asked.

"I'm saying this woman was beaten and stabbed repeatedly with a pair of scissors. I'm not so sure her murder has anything to do with Brad or the mercenaries. It could just be coincidence that she worked at the funeral home.

"Gloria Chimes's murder was unbelievably violent. This looks like a crime of passion. Not the crime of a trained killer, no matter how inept they are. This took some time. We need to find out everything about this woman we can. Husband, boyfriend, exes..."

"And what if it's not one of those options?" Agatha asked. "What if the remaining mercenary is just ticked we're unravelling all his plans and needed to take it out on someone?"

"I guess that could be a possibility too," Coil said. "And I guess we'd better find him before he does it again."

CHAPTER TWO

Monday

The metal was cool to the touch as Hank wrapped his fingers around the dangling triangle that hung above his hospital bed. He grunted and pulled himself up, his breath catching as pain shot through his ribs and chest.

The damage he'd sustained from falling off of a cliff while searching for Agatha had left him paralyzed from the waist down. He sucked in a deep breath as he muscled his body into a seated position while his fingers fumbled for the big clunky remote clipped to his hospital bed. He turned on the television, and a soap opera flickered to life. He had to get out of this place. He was going crazy.

He stretched his arms and shoulders, fighting through the pain. He'd spent most of his time sleeping, and as long as he stayed ahead of the pain, the aches and pains, bruises and cracked ribs, were more than livable. He could do everything at home that he was doing here.

His appetite was back with a vengeance, and Dr. Sullivan had told him no surgery was necessary. They were just waiting for the swelling to go down around his spine so they could get clear test results. He could wait for his legs to start working again in his own bed.

"Hank Davidson?" a man's voice called from the doorway.

Hank looked away from the TV and used the remote to raise himself to a higher sitting position. The man looked stiff and uncomfortable, and Hank didn't recognize him. He wore a surgical mask and a pair of horn-rimmed glasses, and Hank waited for the man to identify himself.

"I'm with the patient care team here at the hospital."

Hank remained silent. The man wore a white lab coat that stretched across well-developed muscles in his shoulders, chest, and arms. There was no identification badge on his lab coat as far as Hank could tell, and the man stood enough in the shadows and with the hallway light to his back that Hank couldn't see his face clearly.

"You are Hank Davidson?"

"I didn't catch your name," Hank said, instead of answering. "Who are you?"

"I'm with the hospital."

"That's your name?" Hank asked, slipping his hand beneath the covers and wrapping his fingers around his .45.

Hank's intuition was never wrong, and this guy had his Spidey-sense going crazy. The man wore an untucked Polo shirt, and with the lab coat on top of it, Hank couldn't tell if he was armed. But he had a feeling something deadly was holstered under that shirt.

"I just want to make sure I've got the right patient," the guy insisted. "Are you Hank Davidson?"

"No, I'm not," Hank said, faking a smile. "You better check your information at the nurses' station."

The man stood in the doorway, his body tense, and Hank could see the pulse beating in his thick neck.

"You okay, buddy?" Hank asked. "You don't look so good. Maybe you should be the one seeing a doctor."

"Yeah, I'm fine," replied the man. "Are you sure you're not Hank Davidson?"

Hank eased his hand out from beneath the thin white cover and rested the .45 on his lap. The man's expression tightened, and his eyes were glued to the gun.

"Like I said," Hank said. "You've got the wrong guy."

The man didn't flinch, and his hand made a movement as if it was reaching for his own weapon.

"Nope," Hank said, "Keep your hands where I can see them. I'm all hopped up on pain meds, and I'd hate for my finger to slip. Of course, you might have a fighting chance for survival since we're in a hospital. As long as I don't hit you in the head. Brains and .45s don't go well together."

"Relax, buddy," the man said. "You've got the wrong idea. I'm just here to—"

"Save it," Hank said, cutting him off. "We both know why you're here. But the question is, who sent you?"

"The hospital sent me to check on you," the man said, continuing with his farce.

Hank held the gun up and pointed it at the man. "I've been through an ordeal and my patience is running real low, so I'm going to ask you one more time, and then I'm going to shoot you."

The man's eyes became slits. He looked to the left, and Hank knew he was weighing his chances of darting behind the wall before Hank could shoot him.

Hank adjusted his gun slightly. "You want to make a move for cover? Please, give it a shot. You're standing really close, so my chances of missing are zero. Now tell me who sent you."

"I could've made this painless for you," the man said,

not bothering to hide the menace in his voice. "You could have slept right through it. Now you're going to be a problem. And a problem for me means it's going to be painful for you."

"I don't avoid problems," Hank said. "I eliminate them."

"Wrong move, Hank," the man said, holding his hands up. "Take this as a warning. I'm going to finish my assignment one way or the other."

"What's your assignment?" Hank asked.

"I'm batting cleanup." The man made his thumb and first finger into a gun and then mimicked pulling the trigger.

"Uh-huh," Hank said. "And considering I've already met the other morons on your dream team, you can see why I'm not too worried. There will be a lot of people looking for you. There's a reason your friends are dead."

"You must be talking about your girlfriend," he said, sneering. "She was easy to kill. Too bad you weren't there to save her this time."

Hank felt his blood run cold, and if he hadn't just hung up the phone with Agatha not twenty minutes ago, he would've been in a downright panic.

Hank shrugged at the man's boast. "I guess you just saved me a fortune in wedding bills. Do you know how much weddings cost these days? It's outrageous. Who sent you?"

"You think this is a game?" the man asked, his temper getting the best of him. He moved to take a step forward and Hank put his finger on the trigger. The man heard the tiny click it made that signaled things were about to go past the point of no return.

"It's never a game when the lives of my family and friends are on the line. Haven't you ever heard the saying, Don't Mess With Texas? The people in this town will mess you up. One of your buddies got shot by an old woman in the middle of the highway. My fiancée took out two more by herself, and I finished off one of them. Who trained you guys? Tickle Me Elmo? It was the most pathetic thing I've ever seen."

"You sure have a smart mouth for a cripple in the hospital," the man said. "I know what you're trying to do, and it won't work. You're a sitting target. You can't be ready all the time."

"Sure I can, but since I'm the one on the right side of the gun today I'd suggest you be on your way."

"Good morning, Hank," Dr. Sullivan said, sticking his head in the door. "Oh, I didn't realize you had company."

Dr. Sullivan froze when he saw Hank's pistol pointed at the man, and he opened his mouth to yell out the alarm when the man grabbed Sullivan and used his body as a shield so he could escape the room. He shoved Sullivan to the ground at the last second and made his getaway.

"You okay, Doc?" Hank asked, keeping his weapon trained on the door in case the man made a reappearance.

"Holy cow," Dr. Sullivan said, getting to his feet. "What the heck just happened? We need to call the police."

"The sooner the better," Hank said, tossing Sullivan his cell phone. He didn't want to splinter his attention away from the door. "You've got a killer on the loose. Come over on this side of the bed. I can protect you better over here in case he comes back."

Hank hit the alarm button on his remote to alert the nurses' station, and when a woman answered he told her to alert security and to shut down the building. He identified himself as Detective Davidson and fortunately, Dr. Sullivan was there to back up the order.

Dr. Sullivan put 911 on speakerphone so Hank could

give a description of the man. Within minutes the entire medical complex was swarming with cops. SWAT teams flooded every floor and hallway. Hank knew the drill and waited until the tactical units had officially cleared the building, and he made sure to set his badge on the bed in plain view so responding officers would know he was one of the good guys. He kept his weapon out of immediate sight, but still at the ready.

He'd never felt so helpless in his life. Sure, he was protecting Dr. Sullivan, but stuck in a bed hoping for help to come wasn't very brave or courageous. All he could think about as officers maneuvered their way down the hall was how thankful he was that Agatha wasn't there with him.

After Dr. Sullivan had hung up after calling 911, Hank had voice-dialed a call to Agatha to let her know what had happened. She'd already filled him in on what had happened to Gloria Chimes, and if he was lucky, Coil was still with her and she was well protected.

"Aggie," he said when she answered the phone. He hadn't realized how relieved he'd be to hear her voice and know for sure the mercenary hadn't somehow gotten to her. "You're okay?"

"What's wrong, Hank?" she said. "Coil's phone started ringing off the hook, and someone said the SWAT team got called into the hospital. We're on the way there now."

"I think I met the rest of the team," Hank said. "He told me he was batting cleanup. He wasn't too appreciative when I pulled a gun on him, but we haven't seen the last of him."

"Thank God you're all right," she said. "We're pulling into the parking lot now. See you in a few minutes."

A couple of detectives were questioning him and Dr. Sullivan when Agatha and Coil came into the room. Agatha pushed past the detectives and wrapped her arms around his neck. It felt good to hold her, even if it was painful.

"Oh, sorry," she said, releasing him quickly.

"No, it's okay," he told her. "The hug did more than the pain meds."

"Well, looks like you've stirred up a hornet's nest," Coil said, nodding to the detectives.

Hank nodded. "Looks like. The guys we killed at the meatpacking plant must've relayed the information about us to him. He must have been who was coming to extract them. A backup in case trouble arose. He knew I was here. And knew my name. But he didn't have a visual of me. He asked repeatedly if I was Hank Davidson. The way he talked, I got the feeling he's working this alone. There was a feel of desperation. As if he was trying to clean up a lot of messes by himself."

"Lord, if only we could be so lucky," Coil said. "The last thing this county needs is a swarm of hitmen coming to kill everyone."

The female detective—Sergeant Lucy Strong—cleared her throat. She had light brown hair that was short and framed her face, and intelligent brown eyes. She wore pin-striped slacks and a pale blue button-down shirt.

"We're feeling a little out of the loop here," she said. "Maybe you could fill us in since we're not in Bell County. Especially if we're about to have problems in Austin."

"It's a long story," Coil replied. "We discovered a smuggling operation that was being run out of a local funeral home in Rusty Gun. The guy who owned the funeral home was working with hired mercenaries to ship weapons down into Mexico."

"Weapons in the bodies?" Strong asked, her brows raised high.

"Explosives," Coil said.

"The morgue in Bell County," Strong said, nodding. "I saw it on the news. You lost one of your own."

"Yeah," Coil said, his mouth grim. "The mercenaries turned on their body supplier at the funeral home and killed him. And by a weird chance of fate, the last body they took fell out of the hearse they were using to transport it and Hank's sisters ran over it. The mercenaries got out and shot at his sisters, but they weren't planning on them shooting back. We figured they were afraid the body would explode so they took off. They were using the meatpacking plant as a base of operations, and they were basically stuck there with a hearse that had a shot-out tire and a rotting corpse in the back until someone came to extract them."

"And that's who this guy is," Strong said, nodding in understanding.

"Right," Coil said. "If Hank hadn't been armed this would be a very different story right now."

Strong smirked. "You do realize you're not allowed to have that weapon in here, right?"

"We'll pretend I'm on duty," Hank said, tapping his badge on top of the blanket. "Besides, I'm checking out today. Dr. Sullivan and I had a good conversation, and I'm pretty sure he wants to avoid being used as a shield again. Isn't that right, Doc?"

"There's nothing we can do for you here that you can't do at home," Dr. Sullivan said. "At least not until that swelling goes down and we can get you back in for tests."

Agatha's eyes brightened. "You're coming home?"

Hank squeezed her hand and nodded.

"I know you're going to be busy with bad guys and guarding your home," Dr. Sullivan said, "But it's important to continue to do the exercises I told you. Keep moving. Stay

17

ahead of the pain. It's going to take hard work to get you back up to full speed."

"Hard work is my middle name," Hank said.

Strong snorted out a laugh. "That's funny, because on my police report you told me your middle name was—"

"Stop," Hank said, laughing nervously. "My middle name is private information."

"Huh," Coil said. "Come to think of it, I've known you for all these years, and I don't think I've ever heard you mention your middle name. What could it possibly be?"

"It's..." Hank paused. "None of your business."

"I know it," Agatha said, winking at Coil.

"Me too," Sergeant Strong teased.

Hank noticed the narrow-eyed glare Agatha shot at Sergeant Strong, and he'd never seen her bare the teeth of jealousy before. Cops were notorious for flirting with each other, and he'd gotten used to ignoring the banter over his career. He was used to it, but Agatha wasn't, and he never wanted her to feel threatened or like she didn't have his whole attention.

He squeezed her hand reassuringly. "Okay, enough about me," Hank said. "We've got more important things to worry about than my middle name."

"Don't think I'm not going to circle back to it though," Coil said.

A man in a tactical dress uniform who was part of the SWAT team had been standing toward the door, and he took a step forward. "Sorry to interrupt the pleasantries, but is this description all you can tell us? He fits in with most of the hospital staff and the general population. Anything distinguishing about him?"

"Good question," Hank acknowledged. "I guess his ability to blend is also what makes him effective. And dangerous, but other than his clothing description, he's just as I described."

"That's not much to go on, sir," the SWAT detective said, clearly displeased.

"I understand, but it's all I can tell you without making something up to satisfy you," Hank replied. "Have you watched the hospital's surveillance feed? Elevators, lobby, stairwells... He had to get in somehow."

"We're reviewing the video now, but so far, no one stands out."

"Watch for his movements," Hank said. "He's military. Overly muscular and very stiff when he moves. He's about six feet and midforties."

"We found another body a couple of days ago in Rusty Gun," Coil said, "and I'd like to question our mystery mercenary about her. She worked at the funeral home where they were getting their body supply."

"Wrong place, wrong time?" Strong asked. "Or was she working with them?"

"I'm thinking wrong place, wrong time," Coil said. "But we'll see how it shakes out once the evidence starts coming in."

Hank knew Coil was bothered by the fact that Gloria Chimes was killed in a different manner than the other victims, and that he wasn't putting all his eggs in the "mercenary did it" basket. But sometimes it was best not to give too much information, especially when outside your jurisdiction.

"Y'all ready to get out of here?" Hank asked. "We've got a murder to solve, and I could use a hamburger."

He knew the mercenary was long gone and the detectives had a job to do. There was nothing more he could offer than what he'd shared. The longer he sat in that hospital, the more risk he was in.

"Hank, we'll let you know if we have any more questions for you," Sergeant Strong said. "So far, it looks like this is probably dead in the water on our end. With you back in Bell County, I doubt we'll see your friend again. But feel free to come back and visit any time," she said, giving him a wink.

"Hank, I'll have your discharge paperwork sent up shortly," Dr. Sullivan said, heading out of the room. "And I'll have someone come by to talk to you both about home health resources."

"He'll need at-home nurses?" Agatha asked.

"Not around the clock, but he's not out of the woods yet," Dr. Sullivan said. "Hank's injury is very serious, but he'll rest better at home. The less stress you have and the more rest you get, the faster your body will heal. Besides, it's probably a lot safer with you out of here."

"You're going to hurt my feelings, Doc," Hank joked.

"My heart can't take that kind of action," Dr. Sullivan said. "But I'm still coming to your wedding. I heard the menu is going to be out of this world, and you've got an open bar."

"Glad we can oblige," Hank said.

Dr. Sullivan chuckled and waved on his way out, and the officers followed him out. Hank and Agatha didn't have to wait too long before a nurse came in with his discharge papers and a number to call to get home health set up.

Once all the paperwork was signed, she unhooked his machines and took out the IV, moving the wheelchair close to the bed so he could be maneuvered more easily.

"I rode with Coil," Agatha said, smacking her hand on her forehead. "How are we going to get home?"

"Oh," the nurse said. "Your ride is waiting in the semi-circle out front."

"My ride?" Hank asked.

The nurse just smiled and then took the signed paperwork with her out the door. Agatha rolled Hank down the hall to the elevator, and then out of the elevator to the lobby once they reached the bottom floor.

He saw the old silver minivan sputtering in front of the double doors, and he started shaking his head in denial. It was his sisters. Hazel was behind the wheel and Patsy opened the sliding door and got out, looking both ways before motioning them to come outside. Hank noticed Patsy was wearing a weapon at her waist, and dollars to donuts Hazel was too. They looked like a senior citizen's secret service detail.

He was starting to think he was better off at the hospital dealing with the mercenary that wanted to kill him.

CHAPTER THREE

Agatha could have kissed Coil. Just as they got Hank and his wheelchair loaded up in the van, Coil pulled up behind them in his truck. The look on her face must have been pretty pathetic because he offered to drive her back to Rusty Gun since he was headed in that direction.

She did feel a little bad about leaving Hank alone with his sisters, and her lips twitched when she saw the expression on his face when they pulled up in front of her and Hank's house. She thought he was going to jump out of the van as soon as the door opened, despite the fact he couldn't walk.

Coil must have noticed it too because he said, "Man, are you going to be in trouble."

"I'm willing to take my chances," Agatha said. "Thanks for the ride."

"I had some of the guys come over and make some modifications to the house," Coil said. "I didn't figure y'all would think about it with everything going on."

Agatha felt tears prick her eyes as she noticed the ramp

leading up to the porch and a new front door that was wider than their old one.

"Oh, wow," she said. "I don't even know what to say. I didn't even think—"

"That's what friends are for," Coil said, patting her awkwardly on the shoulder. "You'd better go rescue Hank. He doesn't look so good."

Coil was right. Hank looked terrible. His skin was an odd shade of green, and he was hunched over, hanging halfway out the door.

"You okay, baby?" Agatha asked.

"I need my gun," Hank gasped out.

"Your gun?" Agatha asked. "Why?"

"Someone needs to be put out of their misery," Hank said. "I'm not sure if it's them or me."

"There you go," Agatha said. "You've kept your sense of humor. Come on, big guy. You'll feel better once we get you in the house."

"How does Hazel still have a license?" Hank asked. "She ran that FedEx truck right off the road, and she hit three trash cans. We could've died."

"Man, the hospital made you soft," Hazel said, shaking her head. "You were perfectly safe. I was just trying to shake some feeling back in your legs."

Hank grunted and let Coil help get him maneuvered into the wheelchair. Agatha noticed he was silent as he took in the changes to their front porch, and the air felt heavy around them as she pushed him up the sidewalk and into the house.

They got Hank settled into his recliner in front of the TV and the big picture window that looked out over the street.

"We're being watched," Hank said. "That blue sedan has made two passes on the street."

"I hope so," Coil said. "You've got round the clock protection here. I talked to a couple of the chiefs of local police departments, and they're willing to help us out by having officers do drive-bys. We've got your sisters covered too."

"Isn't that sweet," Betty said, smiling vacantly. "Lordy it's hot outside. I'm due for my afternoon gin and tonic." She looked right at Agatha and said, "You'd be surprised how refreshing it is. I drank them all the time when I was going through menopause. Those hot flashes never stood a chance. You remember that, dear. That's good advice."

Agatha *hmm*ed noncommittally. She liked Betty the best of all Hank's sisters. She was something of a flake, but she had a kind heart and she loved Hank.

"You're hurting," Agatha said, narrowing her eyes at Hank. "You're supposed to stay ahead of the pain, and you've overdone it with all the excitement at the hospital today. Time for a pill."

"They make me sleepy, and I need to keep watch."

"No," Coil said, stepping in. "You need to do what the doctor said and let your body heal. You've got a wedding coming up. We've got your six, brother. Don't you trust us?"

"That's a low blow," Hank said. "Fine. I'll take the pills."

Agatha handed him two white pills and an open bottle of water, and she spent a few more minutes making sure he had a soft blanket and the remote was within arm's reach.

Hank was passed out before she could finish covering him up.

"Welp," Hazel said. "Looks like our work here is done. If Betty doesn't get her afternoon drink she gets real cranky, so we've got to be going. They've got bingo at the resort tonight."

Agatha wished them luck and locked the door behind them. Coil was chuckling to himself when she turned around.

"I've never been more glad to be an only child," he said.

"No kidding," she agreed. "I think there's tea in the fridge."

"There's everything," he said. "You know how this town is. You've got more casseroles in the freezer than you're going to know what to do with. Martha Watson made a homemade cherry pie."

Coil looked so pathetic she laughed and said, "I'll cut you a piece. That's sweet of everyone to pitch in like that. I haven't watched the news. I have no idea what's been going on."

She cut a slice of pie for each of them and poured two glasses of tea, and they took a seat on barstools at the kitchen island. She couldn't remember the last time she'd eaten, and she decided she should probably eat a couple of the finger sandwiches she saw on a plate in the fridge with her dessert.

"I need to ask you something," she said to Coil.

"Shoot."

"Do you think we should go through with the wedding on Friday?" She couldn't bear to look him in the eyes when she asked. Now that she'd said the words aloud, it somehow made the possibility that they'd never be married more real.

Coil blew out a breath. "I'm not sure I'm the person to give you that answer. There's always going to be murder. Shelly hates the hours, but loves the job security. So it's not like you can keep putting the wedding off until we're not in the middle of a murder investigation. Does this have to do

25

with Hank's paralysis? Have you changed your mind about marrying him now that he might not walk again?"

Agatha gasped. "Of course not. I'm not that shallow."

"Sorry," Coil said. "I had to ask."

"But we are in danger," she said. "What if this guy isn't caught before the wedding?"

"We can play the 'what if' game all day," Coil said. "But we're going to catch this guy, and we're going to keep everyone safe. Maybe you should ask Pastor Sean what he thinks. We want him and everyone else to feel safe."

She nodded, and dropped her head down onto the island, her food forgotten. It was all starting to hit her, and her shoulders shook with sobs she couldn't contain.

"I'm being selfish," she said. "We should call it off. What's the difference if we get married next month or next year? We love each other and we're together. There's no need putting anyone else at risk. Enough people have died."

"You need to sleep," he said. "Your body and your brain are way past exhaustion, and now isn't the time to make major life decisions. But we all care about you and Hank, and we'll all be there to celebrate your wedding whenever you decide to do it. But just hold off on that decision for a little while."

"Okay," she said. "I'll sleep on it."

"Good because I need you sharp right now with Hank out of the action. You're a good detective, and we're down a man with James gone. I need you to help me focus on the facts. We've got a murder to solve and a killer to catch, and you've got all the things that come with planning a wedding."

"Busy week," she said, her smile weak.

"You need to learn to delegate," Coil said. "Heather has been married plenty of times. She can finish up the loose ends. When Hank needs babysitting while we're working the case I'll send an officer over to replace you. The resort has everything under control for the reception." He grinned. "It takes a village."

She laughed and took a bite of pie, letting it melt in her mouth. It had either been way too long since she'd eaten or that was the best thing she'd ever had. The sugar was starting to rush through her veins, and she knew the extra energy would only last so long before she crashed.

"Anything new on Gloria's murder?" she asked.

"The medical examiner estimates time of death early Saturday morning," Coil said. "There's no sign of forced entry, so he probably waited until she opened up and then walked in and locked the door behind him. With the amount of damage done to her he was probably in there a while. She didn't have a chance to fight back. The ME didn't find any DNA under her nails. He hit her fast and hard and then he kept at it until his fists got tired, and then he finished her off by stabbing her thirty-two times."

"That's a lot of rage," Agatha said, shaking her head.

"Cause of death was blunt-force trauma to the head. She was dead before he started cutting her."

"You don't think it's possible the guy who killed Gloria Saturday is the same guy who tried to kill Hank at the hospital today?"

"There's always a possibility," Coil said.

"But how did he find Hank in the hospital?" Agatha asked. "How'd he find out his name? The mercenary couldn't have been working alone, even though he said he was the last one. He's moved too quickly for that. Someone has to be feeding him information—names and addresses."

"Good point," Coil said. "And I agree with you. I do believe Gloria's murder is connected. It's no coincidence she worked for Brad. We can't rule out the possibility that maybe she was working with them and she was just a loose end. Like you and Hank. Operations like this require a team, a lot of cash, and an even bigger payout. Money makes people do stupid stuff."

"So does fear," she said. "Did Brad have any other employees?"

"Not full time," he said. "Everyone he used was pay for hire, but we're slowly running them down and running background checks on them."

"What about Gloria's ex-husband?"

"Just a baby daddy," Coil said. "His name is Jarvis Turner. He lives in Temple and works for some startup IT company based in San Antonio."

"Does he have a criminal history?" she asked.

"Minor skirmishes. Drunk and disorderly and a DUI. Nothing that shows a propensity toward violence."

Her head was lolling forward, and her eyes were starting to cross.

"I think your sugar rush is over," Coil said. "Go to bed, and I'll fill you in tomorrow. Karl is going to take watch tonight, and he'll be here to help Hank if he needs it."

"Thanks, Coil," Agatha said, sliding off the barstool and shuffling toward her bedroom. "I owe you one."

CHAPTER FOUR

Tuesday

"Can I have seconds?" Hank asked, holding out an empty bottle of Ensure and his banana peel.

"I guess that means you're feeling better," Agatha said, taking them from him and tossing them in the trash. "I'll get you another."

Hank was a creature of habit, and he had to have an Ensure and a banana within minutes of opening his eyes each morning. He figured it lined his stomach so he could have a real breakfast at the café, but in reality, he just didn't like change and he was too stubborn to stop.

And normal seemed important right now. He looked down at his legs, strapped into the footrests of his wheelchair. For some reason, he'd thought he'd wake up this morning and he'd be fully functioning again. Instead, Agatha was waiting on him and the home health nurse was coming to help him shower and dress.

"I feel better today," he told Agatha. "I don't need the pain meds."

She stared at him for a few seconds and must have been

satisfied he was telling the truth because she went back to organizing food and other things people kept bringing by the house.

There was something going on with Agatha, but he couldn't put his finger on it. He knew she was worried about him, but she was more distracted than usual and she seemed...sad.

"Is everything okay?" he asked.

"Of course," she said. "Why wouldn't it be?"

He narrowed his eyes, knowing his intuition had been correct, because she'd looked guilty as sin when she'd answered him.

"I won't be in this wheelchair forever," he said.

"Oh, I know," she said. "I think once your body gets the rest it needs and the swelling goes down, you'll be back on your feet in no time."

That rang true, so he guessed it wasn't his paralysis that was worrying her. He decided to keep probing.

"You nervous about the wedding?" he asked. "Lots to do before Friday."

Her hands stilled, and her eyes got that deer in the headlights look. *Bingo.*

"What's going on, Agatha? You can talk to me about anything. I love you."

She let out the breath she'd been holding. "I love you too. Do you think we should wait? Everything seems so uncertain right now. There's someone out there right now looking to kill us both."

Hank's lips twitched. "To my way of thinking, that just makes me want to get married sooner. I want you to be my wife. No matter the time or the place. If you want to hold off on things for a while, I'm fine with that. Though I'll admit it's getting harder and harder to live in the same house with you and just be roommates. And I was kind of looking forward to Friday because I've never been a good dancer and I figured me being in this chair would keep me off the dance floor."

She chuckled and leaned in to kiss him. "We'll worry about the wedding later. We're both so bruised and battered looking I'm not sure makeup is going to work. I might have to find a dress that covers me from neck to ankles."

"I can't wait to see you in your dress," Hank said. "And I don't care how bruised you are. We'll look back on those pictures twenty years from now and remember that we survived, and because we survived, we were able to spend the rest of our lives together."

"Wow, aren't you Mr. Romantic," she said, tears pricking her eyes. "I think I like those pills you've been taking."

"Very funny," he said.

"And since you're in such a good mood this morning, Coil wants you to come to the sheriff's office today so you can go through Gloria Chimes's case file. He really needs your help. The hospital and insurance has gotten everything set up. We've got a rental van that's wheelchair accessible, and Coil says he's got a comfortable place set up for you to work. He figured you'd be going stir crazy about now."

"He'd be right," Hank said. "As long as I get fed at regular intervals I can be the Energizer Bunny."

"We'll see how that's working for you in a couple of hours," she said. "I'll bring your pills just in case. The nurse is here, so you can go clean up, and I'll do the same. I'll meet you back here in twenty minutes."

When the nurse wheeled Hank back into the living room he was only five minutes later than he'd told Agatha. She was standing in front of the picture window, dressed in her usual attire of yoga pants, a Buc-ee's T-shirt, and a bright red sweatshirt hanging around her waist. Her hair was up in a complicated-looking knot on top of her head, and her attention was focused on something at the front of the house.

"Well, I have good news and bad news," Agatha said.

"What's the bad news?" Hank asked.

"I think it's better if I show you," she said. "Sure you don't want to take one of those pain pills?"

She opened the front door and pushed him out onto the porch.

"What in the world?" Hank asked, panic starting to set in. "I thought you said we had a rental van."

"We do," she assured him.

Hazel had parked in the front yard again, and he figured he'd have to get new sod by the end of the summer if she kept at it.

"There he is," Hazel said, her voice gruff.

"You look much better," Gayle said. "Did you know your neighbor next door is single? Maybe when you're all better you could invite him to dinner one night and we could get introduced more properly."

"He's thirty," Hank said. "I think he's probably going to be busy."

He heard Agatha snort out a laugh behind him.

"You're looking much better this morning," Betty said approvingly.

Brenda *hmmph*ed. "His legs still don't work."

"Be nice, Brenda," Betty said.

"You just caught us on the way out," Hank said. "We've got a busy day ahead of us."

"That's what we figured," Hazel said. "We're here to help."

"Help with what?" Hank asked. "I'm going into the sheriff's office to look over some case files. Boring stuff."

"Not to us," Patsy said. "You're going to need our help on account of how your brains probably aren't too sharp due to the pain meds."

Patsy considered herself an amateur detective, and she was addicted to crime shows.

"I'm just reading case files," Hank insisted.

"Sounds exciting," Patsy said. "We're going to keep our eye on you. You're in danger, young man, and who better to protect you than your own kin? We even managed to shake that tail on the way over here."

"What?" Hank and Agatha asked together.

"I've been tailed by better," Hazel said. "Coil put those plainclothes officers on us, but I can spot a cop a mile off. I know how to evade the po-po with the best of them. Come on, Hank. Time's a wastin'. You hitching a ride with us or are we riding security detail?"

"Ah," Hank said. "We've got a van."

"Then we'll see you at the sheriff's office," Hazel said. "I sure hope that Coil has some decent coffee."

"I brought my Bailey's just in case it's the cheap stuff," Betty said, patting her bag.

"Good thinking," Hazel said.

The ride to the sheriff's office was much too short, and Agatha parked around back next to Coil's truck, and Hazel muscled the van in one of the other spaces reserved for deputies. Hank sighed. It wouldn't do any good to tell them to move.

"You're looking better," Coil said, coming out to greet them. "I was worried when Agatha said you wanted to come in and work."

Hank's lips twitched. "I thought it was your idea."

Coil cleared his throat and looked at Agatha. "There's a rumor you're having lunch catered."

"Oh, sure," Agatha said, narrowing her eyes at Coil. "It's the least I can do since Coil was so insistent you come in today."

"What's going on?" Hank asked. "I don't need a pity party. You don't have to placate me. If I'm in the way here, I can just go home."

"Oh, no," Coil said, slapping him on the shoulder. "This is the best place for you to be. I don't have to spare any guys to be at your house all day, and I've got an extra set of eyes on the mounds of paperwork this nightmare of a week has generated."

"I guess when you put it that way, I'm essential," Hank said.

Coil pushed him up the ramp and typed in the code for the back door.

"You know," Hank said. "I've been thinking. We know these guys were military. The weapons they used, bullet casings...everything they'd done so far tells a story, and that story had to start somewhere. I've got a contact—"

But he was interrupted as Coil wheeled him through the door and a crowd of people yelled, "Surprise!"

Hank jerked backward, his head hitting Coil in the stomach, and he heard his friend grunt on impact.

"Happy bachelor party," Coil said. "As your best man, it's my responsibility to make your remaining days as a bachelor as painless as possible."

Agatha elbowed Coil in the ribs. "Let's not get too carried away."

"A bachelor party?" Hank asked, his brain not quite catching up. Maybe he was still drugged.

"Technically it's a bachelor and a bachelorette party,"

Gayle said. "Miss Goody-two-shoes is too scared to let us take her out and show her a good time. They've got one of those honky-tonks close by where you can dance on the bars."

"I've always wanted to do that," Brenda said, "But my hips aren't what they used to be."

"It's all right," Gayle said. "These desks are lower to the ground than a bar. I'm sure that handsome deputy over there will help you get your hips moving."

"I should've taken the pain meds and passed out," Hank said.

"I've got them in my purse," Agatha said. "I could sell them to everyone in this room and make a fortune."

CHAPTER FIVE

Wednesday

"How's my favorite almost-husband?" Agatha asked the next morning.

"Ahh, so does that mean we're still getting married Friday?"

"Yes, which makes me very motivated to get to the bottom of whoever that man was who threatened you in the hospital."

"I've been thinking about that," Hank said. "I started to say something yesterday when we got to the sheriff's office, but after Brenda starting dancing, my brain shut off."

Agatha chuckled and kissed him on top of the head. "It was a good party. No one got hurt or arrested, and the cake was delicious. We've got good friends."

"We do," Hank agreed. "And my sisters mean well. Some of the time."

"What were you thinking about the case?" Agatha asked.

"I was saying that these guys being military should give us a little insight," he said. "We've already determined they're not great at their job. They're just trained enough to be dangerous, but inept enough not to be special forces or anything of that caliber."

"Good luck digging into the military side of things," Agatha said. "They like to keep things close to the vest."

"I've got a friend at the Pentagon who owes me a favor," Hank said. "I was thinking there's a possibility these guys were dishonorably discharged or showed deviant behavior while in the military. The military likes to keep an eye on people like that. We need to ask ourselves why we're alive."

"I don't understand," she said.

"We were shot at by a sniper from an elevated position," Hank said. "Any fool with a scope and the right weapon would have hit us easily. But they didn't have the right equipment. Which means whatever level of military they were it was basic. They're not trained in advanced weapons. You and I both could've made shots from that distance with the right weapon."

"But what about the Navajo code they were using to communicate? Wouldn't that signify advanced training?"

"Not really," Hank said. "Anyone can learn the language if they want to. It's not widely used anymore. More of a novelty for guys like this who want to think they're important. I sent all the information about the weapons that were confiscated from the meatpacking plant to my contact to see if he can give us any insight. I also sent him the fingerprints and the blood sample we collected off the highway after Hazel shot him. His DNA and prints will be in the system if he's one of theirs."

"Have you heard back from him?"

"He said the weapons I asked about are not standard military issue," Hank said. "I believe the word he used was junk."

"It seemed deadly enough when bullets were flying past my face," Agatha said dryly.

Hank nodded. "I'm still waiting to hear back from him about the forensics matching. Maybe we need to take a look closer to home. We need to look further into Brad's past. Maybe their connection is deeper than just a work for hire. College buddies. Childhood friends. Brad was never in the military, but Coil said he went to the University of Texas. Maybe Brad met them there. We need to dig deeper into Gloria Chimes's past as well. Maybe she's the one connected to the mercenaries and not Brad."

"You're very attractive when you're thinking," Agatha said.

"What?" Hank asked, looking up in surprise.

"You get this cute little line right between your brows," she said, touching it gently. "So serious. Maybe we shouldn't wait until Friday to get married. It seems so far away."

Hank laughed and pulled Agatha toward him so she lost her balance and fell into his lap.

"*Oomph*," he said and winced.

"Oh no," she said, scrambling to get up. "I didn't mean to hurt you. Are you okay?"

"I felt that," he said. "When you fell in my lap. I felt it."

"Are you sure?" she asked. "Can you move your legs?"

Hank concentrated for a moment, and frustration marred his brow. He'd felt the pain for that brief instance, but he couldn't make his legs move.

"Can you feel this?" Agatha said, placing her hand on his thigh.

Disappointed, Hank said, "No."

"How about this?"

This time Agatha balled up her fist and punched him. He burst out laughing.

"Let's not make it a habit, but there was some sensation."

"That's a great sign," she said excitedly. "This is cause for celebration. How about pie?"

"I'll never say no to that," Hank said, checking his email to see if his contact had gotten back to him. He saw the email come up, and opened it quickly. "Speak of the devil."

"What was that?" Agatha asked, bringing in two plates of pie and two glasses of tea on a tray.

"My contact emailed back," he said. "The DNA samples I sent are coming up negative for a match. That's strange."

"Why don't you refer to your contact at the Pentagon by his name?" she asked. "Is it a big secret or something?"

"Yes," Hank said.

"Yes, what?"

"Yes, it's a big secret," he replied.

"What's the secret?" she pressed.

"Who the person is at the Pentagon."

"Why?"

"Because—"

"Because why?"

"Because it is," he said, shrugging. "Who the person is isn't important. But what he shares with me because I'll never identify him is very important. See?"

"Got it," she said. "So what does that mean if the DNA sample doesn't match what's in the military database?"

"It means I was wrong about the man Hazel killed as being one of our soldiers," he said. "Because if he'd been in our military my contact would've gotten a hit. My contact did come back with something helpful though."

"What's that?" Agatha asked.

"He recognized a tattoo from the autopsy photos on our mercenary's back. It's an insignia used by the Croatian Army. It didn't take him long to do a little digging, and it turns out this man matched the description of a Croatian officer who'd been sent to the United States for advanced military training with several other officers.

"The rest of his team came home, but apparently, our merc enjoyed the American way of life a little too much, and he decided to overstay his welcome and go AWOL. The Croatian Army did a cursory search, but they didn't put too much time or resources into locating him."

"I bet it's because of a woman," Agatha said.

"A woman?" Hank asked.

"I'd put money on it," she said. "A man doesn't give up his country and family because he likes fast food and Texas sunsets. Freedom is one thing, but love is another. Once he fell in love and decided to go AWOL, he basically had to go into hiding. And you can't work a regular job when you're in hiding. Of course, being in love also requires money."

"You're telling me," Hank said. "Thank God our reception is free. I don't even want to think how much that would've set us back."

"Let's put it this way," Agatha said. "We've got a very healthy down payment for that land and house we were talking about."

"Don't forget the chickens," Hank said.

"We should have a few dollars left over for chickens," Agatha assured him. "Anyway, doesn't it make sense? You said the rest of his team went back to Croatia, but what if he met some of our own soldiers while on base?"

"It makes sense," Hank agreed. "But it's all supposition at this point. We need facts. I've got a name, so that's where we'll start. We need to find out what base he did his training at, and a list of soldiers stationed there at the time. That's going to be trickier information to get."

"Wow, your contact must owe you a heck of a favor," Agatha said.

Hank just smiled. In truth, his contact owed him his life. "Our merc's name is Ivan Marko. It shouldn't be too hard to get identification on the others. I'm especially curious to know who my friend in the hospital is."

"Does your secret friend at the Pentagon have an address or idea where Ivan Marko might've been shacking up?" she asked.

"The Croatian team went to Fort Hood Army Base in Killeen, Texas," Hank said. "He attended infantry and artillery training, and although it was more advanced than he would've ever known back in his home, it was by no means special operations caliber."

"That's right here in Bell County," Agatha said. "It couldn't have been any easier, could it? No wonder they hid out at the meatpacking plant. I bet they all lived in the area."

"Right under our noses," Hank said. "At least we don't have to search the world to find the last one. We're practically neighbors, and I'm sure Coil will have a good idea of where they operated now that we have one identified."

"But how does a lovestruck foreign national who connects with bottom-dweller soldiers—sorry, I'm having a hard time even thinking of these jerks as part of our military—start using bodies to smuggle explosives?" she asked.

"There are bad seeds in every position and profession," Hank said. "People like to think that we can all be unified if everyone just loves each other and gets along, but the truth is, there's evil in the world and no amount of love and hugs is going to change that. But I agree with you, guys like these smear all the good our men and women in uniform do."

"You ready to go into the office?" Agatha asked. "I feel bad about staying home and taking deputies off the job to keep checking on us."

"Agreed," Hank said. "Springer should've gotten the subpoenaed bank information by now for Sweet Dreams Funeral Home."

"And on the way we can stop by the clerk of courts office and pick up our marriage license."

"Oh, yeah," Hank said. "I totally forgot about that. I guess we need it, huh?"

"Only if we want to make it legal," she said.

CHAPTER SIX

"If it isn't the Davidsons," Coil said, greeting them as Agatha rolled Hank into the sheriff's office.

The name caught Agatha off guard. She'd been Agatha Harley her whole life and being Agatha Davidson was going to take some getting used to. The reality was starting to set in that in two days she was going to be a married woman. Maybe she should hyphenate. Agatha Harley-Davidson. Or maybe not.

She was sweating in places best left unmentioned, and she was pretty sure the temperature outside was breaking new records. She was surprised Hank's wheels hadn't melted to the concrete sidewalk.

"Y'all get in here before you let all the cold air out," Coil said. "You've both got that look in your eyes like you're bursting at the seams to tell me something."

"I'll let Hank do it," Agatha said. "He's the one with the secret contacts."

"Ahh," Coil said. "Must be the Pentagon."

"How in the world did you come to that conclusion?" Agatha asked.

"We're dealing with ex-military. And Hank's got contacts in every agency all over the country. I was just connecting the dots."

Hank filled them in on what his contact at the Pentagon shared. "The man Hazel shot has been identified as Ivan Marko. He was a Croatian soldier who came here with a team for advanced training at Ft. Hood. His team went back to Croatia, but Ivan went AWOL.

"I'm waiting on a list of everyone who was stationed at Ft. Hood during that time. We're going to have to run them all down. It's going to be time consuming. But we do know the guys we killed at the meatpacking plant and the one who came for me at the hospital are American. The rest of the Croatian soldiers that came with Marko are all accounted for.

"We might be looking for a local boy, considering that meatpacking plant isn't exactly on the Bell County tourist map. It's really only known to locals who've been here awhile. It's been a couple of decades since that thing has been in use."

"Don't forget the woman," Agatha said.

"What woman?" Coil asked.

"Agatha has a theory that Marko went AWOL for a woman."

"That's usually the reason men do stupid things," Coil agreed.

"So what should we do until you get that list from your contact?" Springer asked.

"Did the subpoenaed financial data on the funeral home come through?" Hank asked.

"Got it right here," Springer said, holding up a thick file folder. "What should I be looking for?"

"Unusual patterns of cash flow to start with," Hank

said. "But it'll eventually start to look more consistent as bodies were smuggled more frequently. You'd mentioned shielded bank accounts once before, but I wouldn't rule out the obvious."

"Like what?" Springer asked.

"Like a regular service provided by the funeral home—crematoriums, limo services, tent rentals, burial plots—things like that. If you weed out the regular transactions that might leave you with the not so regular. Does that make any sense?"

Springer nodded and said, "Got it."

"Any breaches of security?" Hank asked Coil.

"There's been nothing suspicious reported, and our deputies have kept a loose patrol around your home. It's been four days since the last mercenary made contact with you in the hospital. My guess is that either he's bailed on the mission or he doesn't have the support resources to have tracked down your home address."

"The house is listed under a trust instead of my name," Hank said.

"You think we're safe now?" Agatha asked.

"I wouldn't say safe, but if it was me I'd keep an eye right where we are," Hank said. "If he was able to find out my name and the hospital I'd been taken to, then I'm sure he's been able to find out my background or look at any recent news reports. It's no secret about my ties with the sheriff's office and Coil."

"We'll beef up patrols locally," Coil said. "If he's right under our noses we'll find him."

Hank wasn't having any luck doing searches for Ivan Marko, so he did what any detective would do and logged into his fake social media account. He'd tracked more leads down through social media than he'd ever imagined when he began as a serial-killer tracker for the FBI.

Nothing popped up under Ivan Marko, so he mixed up search combinations of name and location. Finally, after scrolling through hundreds of social media pictures of bathroom selfies and best-life poses, he hit pay dirt by doing a basic search on the meatpacking plant.

It was a family-owned operation that started in the 1920s and passed down through the generations until the late nineties when a fire broke out in one of the processing rooms and destroyed most of the equipment. The family wasn't properly insured, so they had no choice but to close it down.

"The Watson family," Hank said, scrolling through pictures of the fire and tax records. Then he came across a newspaper clipping that showed a picture of a man and a young girl watching their legacy burn to the ground. It was a sad and stark photograph of a family who had just lost everything.

He kept scrolling until he found the name of the man in the photo—George Watson—but after the newspaper story of the fire, information on the Watson family became scarce. In fact, he couldn't find anything else about them. Not tax records or a home address. It was like they disappeared off the face of the planet.

He rolled out of the little office and went next door where Springer was still poring over financial records.

"Springer, can I interrupt you for a minute?"

"Sure thing, boss," Springer said.

"I ran into a snag when I started researching the meatpacking plant," Hank said. "It's been owned by one family for generations, and then they had a fire that destroyed the business. They shut everything down and it's been a ghost town ever since."

"So what's the problem?" Springer asked.

"I can't find any mention of the family over the last twenty years. It's like when the meatpacking plant died, they did too. I have a hunch they might be involved somewhere."

"You've got a name, right? Maybe run a background check through the system."

"I can't run a background check on a hunch," Hank said. "I'd need more than that to run them through the system."

"Well, then your next best bet is Heather Cartwright."

"I beg your pardon?" Hank asked, making Springer chuckle.

"She knows everything about everyone in this town, and all the history that goes with it," Springer said. "She might not have been born here, but she's made up for it. You'd think her family has been here for generations."

"Huh," Hank said, and then rolled back to his own workstation.

He tried calling Heather, but after the third try, he gave up and texted Karl instead. It only took a few seconds before he responded that Heather was over at the Taco and Waffle.

Agatha was busy doing her own work, and he wasn't about to ask help from any of the other officers at the sheriff's office. He could throw a rock and hit the Taco and Waffle from where he was, so surely he could roll himself across the street without any help.

He sucked in a deep breath and then rolled himself to

the front door. He'd not quite gotten the hang of opening doors and wheeling himself out at the same time, so it took him a minute to maneuver himself across the threshold. By the time he finally got through the door he was dripping with sweat and out of breath. And he really hoped no one had witnessed it.

He shielded his eyes against the blazing summer sun and rolled down the ramp and onto the sidewalk. His teeth knocked together as he navigated the broken concrete and missing pavers as he crossed the road.

He spotted Heather's two-seater sports car parked in front of the Taco and Waffle. It was illegally parked, but what else was new?

By the time he rolled into the Taco and Waffle, he didn't even feel the cold A/C against his skin. He was sick to his stomach, and he thought he might pass out.

"Hank, is that you?" Heather said, bending down so she could look him in the eyes. "You don't look so good."

"I don't feel so good," Hank said.

"What in the world were you thinking, trying to come over here by yourself? What if you'd gotten hit by a car or something? Agatha can't marry a corpse, buddy."

"Right," Hank said. "I was actually looking for you. You didn't pick up your phone."

"It's probably in the bottom of my purse somewhere," she said. "I'm just waiting on Karl to get here for lunch. He got caught at a traffic stop. What are you looking for me for?"

"I'm trying to find out information about the Watson family. The ones who owned the meatpacking plant. I found a picture of George Watson and his daughter and a newspaper article when it caught on fire, but then it was like they disappeared."

Heather nodded her head and rolled him over to her table. "Maddie, honey, bring my friend a glass of water."

"You got it, Ms. Cartwright," the waitress said.

"That meatpacking plant has never been anything but trouble," Heather said, digging into her chips and salsa. "Old Mr. Watson was a real sourpuss. Lived to be a hundred and four. Agatha and I were kids when he died. He lived in that big white house at the end of Sycamore Street."

"The one all the kids think is haunted?" Hank asked.

"That's the one. He let it run down after his wife died, and nobody ever stepped foot near his property without him coming out to stand on the porch with his shotgun. He shot a couple of chunks out of the road on more than one occasion."

"Sounds like a stellar guy," Hank said.

"His son and grandson didn't fall far from the apple tree," Heather said. "That's his grandson in the picture you saw in the paper. George Senior had already passed on, so it was George Junior who was running the show. That meatpacking plant employed a lot of Rusty Gun's population, and after they went under we thought we might lose most of the town with it. He'd already run the thing into the red before the fire, and he'd dropped all his insurance policies because he couldn't afford to pay them. He also couldn't meet payroll, so it was suspected he'd set the fire himself."

"What happened to him?" Hank asked.

"Murder/suicide," Heather said. "Killed his wife and then himself."

"I didn't find anything in the papers about it," Hank said.

Heather shrugged. "It happened sure as I'm standing

here. It was said the daughter inherited a life insurance policy from her mother, and some relative took her in."

"Does the meatpacking plant still belong to the family?" Hank asked.

"The daughter, I guess," Heather said. "Lots of people have tried to buy it over the years. The land is in a pretty good spot for a development. But no one has been successful."

"You know the daughter's name? There was no record of it that I could find. Not even a birth certificate or obituary listing."

"It started with an *L*," Heather said. "Laura, I think." And then she snapped her fingers. "No, Lorelei. That's what it was. Lorelei Watson. She would've been around eight or nine at the time."

"Was she an only child?" Hank asked.

"Nope, there was an older half brother," Heather said. "He caused a bit of a scandal in his teens. He was special, so they sent him away to some school in Austin, but when he came back home for Christmas one year people's animals started turning up dead. Everyone suspected him, but there was never any proof. And then he went back to school and the killings stopped. He was messed up in the head. Everyone in town talked about him. I was already on my second husband by then, but I remember the gossip."

"And thank goodness for it," Hank said. "You know his name?"

"Sure, it was a weird one," she said. "Jarvis Turner. Never saw him again after that Christmas, but he's made headlines. He owns some hotshot IT company. Computers and stuff. I saw him at a party once when I was married to my fifth husband. All the movers and shakers were there, and so was he. He gave me the heebie-jeebies, and thank goodness he didn't recognize me." She shuddered and took a sip of her lunchtime margarita.

"I told Gloria when she hooked up with him that she was making a mistake, but you know how it is with hormones. There's some things you just have to find out for yourself."

"Wait," Hank said. "Is Jarvis Gloria's ex?"

"Not her ex-husband," Heather said. "That guy is long gone. Jarvis is her baby daddy. She never talks about him much, but I know she was finally able to get him to court and to pay child support. He's loaded, so she ended up doing pretty good. How else do you think she opened up that fancy salon in Rusty Gun?"

"Can you do me a favor?" Hank asked, knowing in small towns police work sometimes had to happen a little differently.

"Anything for my best friend's husband-to-be," she said, giving him a wink.

Heather always knew how to make him feel awkward and uncomfortable. He cleared his throat. "See what you can find out about Lorelei. I want to know if she's still local. What happened to her."

Heather narrowed her eyes. "This has something to do with Gloria's murder, doesn't it? You're not just asking 'cause you're curious. Especially now that you know Jarvis is involved."

"I think it's all related to what happened to me and Agatha back at that meatpacking plant. All the people and pieces are starting to fit together."

"Then consider me deputized," Heather said. "I'll see what I can find out."

Hank winced, but decided not to correct her.

CHAPTER SEVEN

The trek back across the street to the sheriff's office was a lot easier since Heather had been nice enough to wheel him over. And his timing was perfect because Coil and Agatha were both sitting in the conference room with Springer.

The look on everyone's faces when Heather wheeled him through the door was worth the price of admission.

"Don't worry about me, Sheriff," Heather said, letting Hank go so he could wheel himself toward the conference room. "I'll do you proud. I'll do my duty. And if I run into trouble, I've got a brand-new hot-pink Ruger that can take care of business if you know what I mean."

"Uhh," Coil said, but Heather was already back out the door. "Do I want to know what that was about?"

"Probably not," Hank said. "It's best to claim ignorance on this one. I do have some information we need to move on though."

Hank rolled into the conference room with the others and said, "We already know that Ivan Marko came to Ft. Hood to attend a special military training class from Croatia. My contact at the Pentagon sent me a list of everyone stationed at Ft. Hood during the time Marko was there. I do believe, based on the location of the meatpacking plant, as well as the involvement of Gloria and Brad, that we're looking for local boys who know the area. As you'll see, there are eleven Texas boys on my list. We can start running them down by name and date of birth."

"Great job, Hank," Coil said. "I sure wish I knew who your source was at the Pentagon."

"You too?" Agatha asked.

"I've wanted to know for years," Coil said, grinning. "But Hank is a closed book when it comes to his sources."

"Which is why I'm trusted with information," Hank said, arching a brow. "Because I don't blab about my sources."

"Yeah, yeah," Springer said, teasingly. "You sure have a lot of friends in high places."

"My government clearance was high too," Hank said, smiling. "What did you find out, Springer?"

"From what I've been able to decipher," Springer said, "Brad Hartley's funeral business looked legitimate on the surface. There were no suspicious financial transactions, revenue spikes, or patterns to raise a red flag, but the average amounts of his inputs and outputs rose significantly within a short period of time."

"Meaning?" Agatha asked.

"Well, if you signed a big contract or launched a product or service and your business exploded overnight, then you'd see a big increase in revenue as well as an increase in expenses for personnel, materials, marketing, things like that," Springer explained.

"Got it," she said.

"First of all, Hartley shouldn't have been hurting for cash. That funeral home made a fortune, and he filed and paid taxes accordingly, so it looks on the up-and-up from the surface. From the time he took over after his father died, Hartley's records show a steady increase in overall volume.

"So I averaged the amount of expenses Hartley would incur for a funeral. He offers different price point packages to his clients—things like caskets, burial plots, gravediggers, use of the sanctuary, flowers, and hair and makeup. Then I compared it to the amount of revenue he was taking in, and I was able to extrapolate an estimated number of burials he'd have to perform to support that level of expense and revenue. Next, I checked with the social security commission who tracks deaths and burials to see exactly how many people had died and were buried in Bell County."

"That's great work, Springer," Coil said, clapping him on the back.

"Thanks," Springer said, pinkening slightly. "But get this, based on Hartley's financial averages for processing a complete funeral package, he'd have to have buried more than two thousand people to match his shown income."

Agatha whistled. "Two thousand people a year? That's crazy."

"Two thousand people a day," Springer corrected. "He was raking in millions."

"That's more people than are in the entire county," Coil said.

"That's right," Springer said, nodding. "In the last five years, Bell County has averaged one thousand and ninety-one deaths. That includes every gender, age, and cause of death. Even Dallas County averages below eight thousand deaths per year."

"Okay, so Brad Hartley was doing something very illegal and very lucrative," Coil said. "And since he was trying to make things look like they were on the up-and-up, that means he was probably laundering money by paying his contractors. People like Gloria Chimes, who was doing hair and makeup. We need to check out his other contractors. Get warrants for their financials."

"Look specifically for any IT services," Hank said.

"What do you know?" Agatha asked, narrowing her eyes at him. "You never ask specific questions like that unless you've got a hunch."

"My hunch is that Brad had the best technology money could buy. Everything from his security system to his bookkeeping software. And I'm willing to bet it all came from JT Intel."

"How'd you know?" Springer said, showing them what he'd pulled up on his computer screen. "Hartley's been paying them millions."

"Everything ties together," Hank said. "The meatpacking plant was owned by the Watson family. The daughter, Lorelei Watson, still owns the property. Her half brother is Jarvis Turner, who owns JT Intel. And he's also the father of Gloria Chimes's daughter. Gloria Chimes worked for Brad. Now we just need to figure how those four are connected to Ivan Marko and the mercenaries out of Ft. Hood.

"Agatha mentioned a woman being involved as far as Marko's reasoning for going AWOL and not returning to Croatia. I think we need to check and see if there's any connection between Marko and Lorelei. Heather's working on it for me. When information doesn't turn up on the internet then you have to go to the next best thing—small town gossip."

"You're a genius," Agatha told him, leaning over and planting a big, fat kiss on his lips.

"We'll see if it pans out," Hank said. "But you're the one

who thought of the woman angle. So maybe you're the genius."

"All right, all right," Coil said. "You're both geniuses. But what does it all mean?"

"Well," Hank said. "I think we need to take a hard look at Jarvis Turner. He's got the money. And money is power. Everyone else would be just a pawn to someone like him. And according to Heather, there were some problems around Rusty Gun when he was a kid."

"Oh, yeah," Agatha said, her mouth dropping open. "I remember that. He was a creepy kid. He killed all of those animals that Christmas. Slit their throats. It was terrible. He got our neighbor's cat and hung it from their porch."

"I was working undercover in Austin at the time," Coil said, "So I wasn't here for that. But I remember my parents talking about it. He got into the pasture on a neighboring ranch and killed thousands of dollars' worth of livestock. But no one ever saw him do it."

"There was never any proof," Hank agreed.

"No, but everyone knew it was him," Agatha said. "You think he made the connection to the mercenaries through his sister?"

Hank nodded. "I think he probably saw an opportunity. People with that kind of money and brains don't get their hands dirty. They hire others to do it for them and take the fall too. I'd be willing to bet at the end of the day, Brad had no clue what kind of money was being laundered through his funeral home. If Jarvis had access to all the accounts, he would've taken care of everything."

"Hey, Sheriff?" Springer asked. "All this talk about networks got me thinking. JT Intel is the biggest tech company in the state. Who manages our IT network?"

"Good question," Coil said. "It's contracted through the

county government, so it's whoever got the clearance and the bid. I'll put a call in and see what I can find out."

"It would certainly explain how they were able to track down Hank in the hospital," Agatha said. "The only reason we've been safe at home is because Hank has the house listed under a trust instead of his name. But having technology at your fingertips like that is very dangerous for us."

"We need to do this by the book," Hank said. "Let's run down those names from Ft. Hood and start connecting all the dots. Heather is looking for Loralei Watson, and Springer, you need to see if you can make as many connections as possible between all the players and Jarvis Turner. This needs to be tight. He's going to have powerful lawyers and a lot of influence from the higher-ups."

"We might not need Heather to track Loralei Watson," Coil said. "Now that we know she's still the owner of the meatpacking plant, that's enough to justify a warrant and a look into her background and financials. Let's see if we can run her to ground and bring her in."

Agatha looked at her watch. "Y'all will have to start this without us. We've got some appointments that can't be missed."

"Like what?" Hank asked.

"We're getting married in two days," Agatha said. "We need to get our marriage license, and then we're meeting with the preacher tonight."

"What?" Hank asked. "Why? We've got a case to solve."

"I'm going to pretend you're not prioritizing this case over our marriage," Agatha said. "There are other people who can do the work while we take a few hours off."

"How come this is the first I'm hearing about this?" Hank asked.

Agatha rolled her eyes. "This is not the first you've

heard about this. You told Pastor Sean last Sunday at church that we'd meet about the ceremony on Wednesday night. We're supposed to meet him and Ashley for dinner."

"Dinner?" Hank asked. "Oh, right. I remember now."

"You mean since there's food involved?" Agatha asked, arching a brow. "Come on, hotshot. Let's get you in the van."

"You sure are in a hurry to marry me, Agatha Harley," Hank said, giving her a teasing grin.

"I'm just excited about getting to use the master bathroom. You've got that big claw-foot tub."

Hank burst out into laughter at her response. Agatha was anything but boring. He couldn't wait to spend his life with her.

CHAPTER EIGHT

Thursday

"Hank," Agatha called out from the living room. "Mind if I take your car today? Heather and I are going to Austin to pick up my wedding dress, and I don't want to ride with Heather. She's a maniac behind the wheel."

"Sure," he said. "Not like I'm going to be driving it anytime soon."

Hank was still lying in bed staring at the ceiling. He'd been up half the night reading reports and doing research on all the potential players. What he really wanted to do was go back to bed and sleep until noon. But he knew the home health nurses would be coming in soon to get him ready for the day.

The nurses were great, but he was getting tired of them coming in and out of the house to help him do things he'd been doing his whole life.

Agatha knocked on his door and then opened it a crack. "You okay?" she asked. "I'm coming in."

He watched her through bleary eyes, wondering how she always looked so alert first thing in the morning. He'd spent his entire career having to get up early, but he was a night owl at heart. And since he'd retired, he'd enjoyed sleeping late and doing things on his own timetable.

"I'm heading out," she said. "The nurse is here."

"You look really nice," he said, taking in the soft summer dress in bright yellow. "You hardly ever wear a dress."

"This is a nice place," she said. "They frown on yoga pants and baseball caps."

Hank snorted.

"You okay with me leaving you here?" she asked.

Hank waved her off. "Sure thing. Coil is coming by later to pick me up. You girls have fun and be careful not to let Heather talk you into a last-minute bachelorette party."

She snorted. "You don't have to worry about that. I'm still exhausted from the last one."

"I can see you're being careful," Hank said, noticing the subtle bulge under her skirt. No one who wasn't trained to look for it would even notice. "Are you wearing your thigh holster?"

She tugged on the black elastic and Velcro attachment that held her snub nose revolver securely in place.

"There was no room in my clutch for it," she said, grinning. "Better safe than sorry." She moved to the side of his bed and kissed him. "I really feel bad about leaving you today."

"Why, sugar?" He lingered in their hold. "Go get your dress. I know it's going to be beautiful. Besides, I have more than enough work to keep me busy."

"Stay out of trouble," she said, waving goodbye and holding the door open for the nurse.

He let the nurse help him through his morning routine grudgingly, and by the time he'd had his Ensure and banana he was mostly awake. He was sitting in the living room, waiting for Coil, when he got a text from Karl.

Karl and Rodriguez had spent the better part of the evening and night tracking down the men who'd been stationed with Ivan Marko. Karl had cold-called one of the retired officers on his list and hit pay dirt. The lieutenant had said three of the names on Karl's list had multiple disciplinary issues.

Hank felt the excitement coursing through his veins. They were getting close, and it wouldn't be long before they started making arrests.

"Dustin Hobbs, Robby Bowers, Jack Hayes, and Killian Flynn," Hank said, reading the names Karl had sent him. Hank messaged Karl to send over photographs of them as soon as possible, and it didn't take long for the images to come up on his screen.

Hank recognized all of them. Dustin, Robby, and Jack were currently in the morgue because he and Agatha had killed them at the meatpacking plant. But it was Killian who'd come to see him at the hospital and tried to kill him there. Now he had a face and a name.

"Gotcha," Hank said.

The back door rattled, and Hank cocked his head, wondering if he'd misheard. Coil wouldn't normally go around to the back, and Hank looked out the window to make sure he hadn't missed Coil's truck pulling in.

He grabbed his phone to look at the exterior surveillance cameras, but it was too late. The glass on the French doors shattered, and he reached for his pistol that was sitting on the table by the front door. He'd reached instinctively, as if his legs still worked, and his hand clutched the gun at the same moment he fell from the wheelchair and onto the floor.

Hank had seconds to make a decision before the man came out of the kitchen and found him on the floor in the living room. He held tight to his gun and pulled himself across the floor and into Agatha's bedroom, closing and locking the door behind him. He saw the dresser and found the strength from somewhere deep within to push it over so it fell in front of the door.

He knew he was making too much noise, but survival was key. He needed to buy enough time to be able to call it in. Coil was likely to walk right into an ambush if he wasn't careful.

Hank crawled to the bathroom and heard the heavy footsteps outside of Agatha's room, and then the knob rattled as he tried to open the door. Shots fired and wood splintered as his attacker slammed against the door. The dresser slid as the door was shoved again and Hank hurriedly pulled himself the rest of the way into the bathroom and slammed the door shut, locking it behind him.

The locked door wouldn't be enough to stop an armed attacker. His elbows burned as he dragged his body along the floor between the tub and toilet.

"I like a challenge," the man yelled out.

Hank had been in fights for his life before, but he'd never had the disadvantage of not having his legs. It was his mind that had to stay cool. He heard more gunshots as the man must have gotten tired of playing around with the heavy dresser in front of the door. Hank dialed Coil and aimed his pistol at the bathroom door. There was nowhere else for him to go. He had to stand and fight. Or at least fight. Standing didn't look like it was going to happen.

Bullets hit the center of the bathroom door and shattered the tile in the shower, raining ceramic shards down over his head.

"Hank," Coil said when he answered the phone.

"Under attack," Hank said into the phone. "Killian Flynn is his name. He's armed and dangerous."

Another shot rang out and Coil said, "I've got units around the block. I'm on the way."

Coil disconnected and Hank took a two-handed grip on his weapon and aimed at the door. He waited for the man to speak again so he knew where he was standing.

"You dead yet?" Killian asked.

Hank smiled and opened fire, unloading his entire magazine.

His ears rang and the smell of cordite filled his nostrils. He reloaded his weapon, the sound of a bullet being loaded into the chamber seemingly loud in the quiet. And then he waited.

His phone buzzed, and he saw it was Coil. He didn't speak when he answered, but Coil knew he'd picked up the phone.

"We're coming in," Coil said. "Watch your fire."

Hank hit a button on the phone so it beeped and Coil knew he understood the message. He kept his weapon in position aiming straight at the door that had just been deci- mated by gunfire. His heart thudded in his chest, and his breath was coming in short pants. He didn't know if his attacker was dead or alive.

He heard footsteps as Coil and his deputies entered the house, and then he heard the sound of Agatha's bedroom window smashing as Killian Flynn escaped.

"I guess that answers that question," Hank said, aggra- vated that he'd missed him. He called out, "Bedroom," so they knew where to look for him and he heard Coil call his name moments later.

"In here," Hank answered. "Guy went out the window."

Coil barked orders to have his men check the perimeter and see if they could pick up a trail, and then the bathroom door opened and Coil was standing there.

They stared at each other a few seconds before Coil said, "You okay?"

Hank looked down at his useless legs and then back at Coil. "I've been better."

"I can see that," Coil said, mouth twitching.

"You're late," Hank told him.

"I stopped by to pick up your tux."

"There better not be any bullet holes in it," Hank said. "I won't get my deposit back."

"You'd better be glad there are no bullet holes in you," Coil said.

CHAPTER NINE

Agatha and Heather had just gotten to the store to pick up her dress when Hank called and told her what had happened. She ran out of the store and jumped back in the car. Heather had come out a few moments later with the bulky dress bag that held her wedding dress and put it in the trunk, and then they'd sped back to Rusty Gun like O. J. Simpson running from the police.

"Hank!" Agatha yelled, pushing open the front door of the sheriff's office. "Hank!"

"In here," Hank called out from Coil's office.

She didn't wait to hear explanations. She just threw her arms around him to make sure for herself that he was really alive. They rolled backward across the floor in his wheelchair but she didn't care.

"You're okay," she cried, touching his face and his hair. "You're all right."

"I'm all right," he assured her. "It's okay. I'm okay."

"Just let me hold you a minute," she said, and then she looked at Coil. "What happened? How could he have gone there undetected?"

"He must have been watching the house," Coil said. "The nurses leave at the same time every morning. And if they're hooked up with JT Intel, he's going to have ears everywhere. Access to text messages or emails. He probably knew you were heading out of town to pick up your wedding dress."

"I knew I shouldn't have left you alone," Agatha said, looking at Hank.

"We can't live our lives that way," Hank said. "It's not your fault. If you'd been there he probably still would have come. Only one of us might be dead."

"Look on the bright side," Coil said. "We've got his name and his picture, and we're plastering it over every media outlet. He won't be able to pick his nose without someone seeing him."

"Gross," Agatha said. "You're sure? You know who he is?"

Hank nodded. "Karl and Rodriguez figured it out. We know who all of them are now."

"That may be so, but what's going to keep them from coming back into our home? We can't go back there until they're caught."

"We probably don't want to go back for a while anyway," Hank said. "This might be a good time to sell the house and find a house on some land like we talked about."

"That bad, huh?" Agatha asked, grimacing.

"You might want to repair the bullet holes before trying to sell," Coil said. "That tends to scare buyers off."

"Good point," Hank said. "I'll call the resort tonight and see if we can stay in the owner's suite. Robert did tell us we were welcome to use it any time. This seems like as good of a time as any."

"Now that everyone has hugged and feels better," Coil

said. "Maybe we could be briefed in the conference room. I've not been brought up to speed on what Karl and Rodriguez found out last night."

They convened in the conference room and Springer joined them. A couple of minutes later, an excited Karl and Rodriguez came through the back door, their faces shining with sweat and a buzz of anticipation swirling around them.

"What happened?" Coil asked as they came in. Neither of them took a seat.

"We found her," Rodriguez said. "Actually, Heather found her. She was out in the parking lot and we ran into her."

"Whoops," Agatha said, remembering she'd left Heather in the car.

Karl grinned at her. "She looked kind of shell-shocked. She said you were driving like it was NASCAR, and she was still a little unsteady on her feet. Once I got her to calm down a bit, she said she'd gotten a text from one of her contacts who said she'd seen Lorelei Watson over at the Drug Mart. Rodriguez and I ran over there, and sure enough, she was standing in line plain as day. She matched the photograph we got from the DMV."

"Lorelei Watson officially changed her name to Lorelei Turner after her parents' deaths," Rodriguez said. "It's why we couldn't find any record of her, and she was a minor, so her records were sealed. Once we found her name and DMV records, we traced her to an address over on Market Street in Temple. The house is registered under Susan Hobbs."

"Hobbs, Hobbs," Hank said. "Why is that name familiar?"

"It's one of the names I sent you this morning," Karl

said. "Dustin Hobbs was one of the mercenaries killed at the meatpacking plant."

"Right," Hank said. "Is Susan his wife?"

"Mother," Rodriguez said. "Looks like Lorelei has been renting from her. She's done a good job of lying low and building layers so she's harder to find."

"Have you talked to Hobbs's mother?" Coil asked.

"Early this morning," Rodriguez said. "Either she doesn't know much or isn't going to give much away. It was hard to tell. She said the last time she saw her son was six months ago. He told her the military found a good job for him and then he disappeared and she hasn't heard from him since."

"But get this," Karl said. "When we started digging into his background, his last known employer was as a tower technician for JT Intel."

"It all keeps coming back to Jarvis Turner," Hank said.

"Can't we get a warrant for Lorelei's house?" Agatha asked.

"Everything is circumstantial right now," Hank said. "All of these people are loosely associated with the mercenaries we met last week. We can dig into Gloria's finances and go through her home because she was directly connected to Brad, and she's dead. Lorelei owns the meatpacking plant, so we were able to get a warrant to search there and the surrounding grounds. We could stretch a warrant to get access to her cell records. If she's renting a house from Dustin Hobbs's mother, then it stands to reason she knew Dustin."

"Let's run it backward," Coil said. "We've got all the cell phones from the men who were killed at the meatpacking plant. Springer has been going through texts and messages. Now that we have her assumed name, he can look for anything specifically from her to any of the mercenaries. If we can tie her to just one of them it'll be enough to get a warrant for her home and finances."

"What about Jarvis?" Agatha asked.

"We need to have everything wrapped with a nice neat bow before we go after the big fish," Hank said.

"Check Ivan Marko's phone first," Agatha said. "I'm willing to bet Lorelei is the reason he didn't return to Croatia. And she's going to be mighty unhappy to find out he was killed."

"We've got three players left," Coil said. "Lorelei, Killian Flynn, and Jarvis. They're trying to cover their own tail right now and eliminate loose ends. Meaning you and Agatha, and probably your sisters since they took out Marko."

"I have a suggestion," Springer said hesitantly. "I know we're waiting to approach Jarvis Turner until we can lock down all the evidence, but what if we can lure him out?"

"Lure?" Coil asked. "What do you mean?"

"Assuming he is the criminal mastermind, I think he's probably tracking our communications somehow," Springer said. "I know that's what I'd do if I was in his place. We have to assume he knows what we know, and that we're getting close to his sister and Killian. There's a reason he knew Hank was home alone this morning."

"You think someone is feeding him information from the inside?" Coil asked, brows furrowed.

"No, not at all," Springer said hastily. "But I think he'd use his company and his network to tap into our system, including our cell phones. I'm still working to connect the dots between Jarvis, Brad Hartley, and any communications with the mercenary team. I'd say at this point, all we have is a criminal conspiracy unless we can place him as Gloria Chimes's killer."

"How about we smoke out the last mercenary, and if he's unlucky enough to be taken alive, then get him to roll over on Jarvis," Hank suggested.

"Think he'll flip?" Agatha asked.

"There's no honor among thieves," Hank said. "This Killian Flynn is looking at so many felony criminal charges that the death penalty will seem like a summer vacation. His only hope of saving himself is to cooperate."

"How do we do it?" Agatha asked.

"Well, Heather did say she was going to fulfill her duties as a deputy," Hank said, grinning.

"I don't remember making Heather a deputy," Coil said, going a little pale.

"It's a long story," Hank said. "But I think we can use her to lure Flynn in without making it seem too obvious. We need someone who isn't a cop. Agatha, all you need to do is text Heather the details of how we're moving over to the resort, and then we'll set a trap to get him when he comes looking for us."

"Man, that resort must hate y'all," Rodriguez said, shaking her head.

Agatha sighed. "Yeah, I'm starting to think we've overstayed our welcome. How do you suppose we get Heather to go along with this without blowing it?"

"Don't tell her," Coil said. "I think we keep it simple. Agatha can text Heather about going to pick up wedding flowers, or something like that, and make sure she knows Hank will be alone. We'll put everyone in plainclothes so they look like guests, and I'll have a couple of women officers go with Agatha to make sure she's protected and so it looks like a girls' outing."

"It sounds like you've given this some thought," Agatha said.

"I'm always thinking," Coil said, grinning. "I knew we were going to have to smoke them out somehow. I just didn't know how the opportunity was going to present itself. Let me get everything organized and then we'll reconvene," Coil said.

"Sounds great," Agatha said. "But I really do need to get some wedding stuff done today. I've got to meet with the florist and the photographer. And Pastor Sean is going to meet us at the church to let us in."

"It's too dangerous for you to be out by yourself," Hank said.

"I'm armed," Agatha insisted. "And these are things I can't put off. We're getting married tomorrow, and I have no idea if everything is going to happen as scheduled. We're not even getting a rehearsal to run through everything. I'm not someone who overreacts when I'm stressed, but I'm pretty close to my meltdown point."

Hank could hear the rising hysteria in her voice, and knew she was trying to take care of him, the wedding, and work the case at the same time. It was enough to push anyone past the breaking point.

"Maybe Rodriguez could help you out today," Coil said, giving his lieutenant a pointed look. "I'm sure she'd enjoy spending the day in plainclothes."

"I've got a change of clothes in my office," Rodriguez said. "Sign me up for wedding duty. No need to be stressed. You and Hank will get married no matter what. The wedding isn't the final destination. Focus on your marriage. You have a whole life after you say your vows."

"Wow," Agatha said. "Wise words."

She shrugged. "My dad's a marriage counselor. I've got a whole bag of wisdom if you need it."

"I'll remember that," Agatha said, looking wide-eyed at Hank.

Hank winked at her.

"You know, these guys really are dumb," Springer said. "Everyone involved is just being used by Jarvis Turner. He's got the money, and he's got the power to think no one will ever catch him. He's gotten away with who knows what his entire life, starting back when he was a kid. But you're only as good as the people you hire. And those mercenaries were morons. It's been child's play to piece things together. Mostly just legwork on our end. He had to know they'd be caught eventually."

"Child's play," Hank said, rubbing his finger along his chin.

"What is it?" Agatha asked.

"I don't know," he said. "Just a feeling. Back in the day it was believed that terror groups were using video game platforms to securely communicate messages outside of the detection of law enforcement and intel agencies. Non-peripheral-based communication on consoles provided terrorists a path to plan attacks. The low-tech idea proved to be a much more secure way to communicate than using phones, texts, or email. There's been an astonishing lack of electronic information on these guys. We've had to do serious legwork. In-person interviews, DMV searches, lots of paper trails. Maybe we're not thinking low-tech enough."

"I don't know what that means," Agatha said.

"Brad Hartley had a gaming system in his office," Hank said.

"Of course," Coil said, nodding in agreement. "We bagged a gaming system at the meatpacking plant too. The guys were living in that one little space with a generator, and they had a television and gaming system. I didn't think much of it. I figured it was just a way for them to pass the time."

"Can we crack open Brad's console and track the messages?" Hank asked.

"Good idea," Springer said, "But no. That's what made using the video games so secure. But if we can find enough to get a warrant for Lorelei Turner's house from Ivan Marko's cell phone, we can look and see if she's got a similar console."

Rodriguez came back in at that moment dressed in her street clothes. "We've got to go," Agatha said. "We've got a full day ahead of us."

Hank grabbed her hand and pulled her down for a kiss goodbye. "I'm sorry I can't help you more with the wedding. You know I would if I could." He tried not to let the uselessness of his legs get to him, but seeing the stress and worry on Agatha's face doubled the guilt he felt.

"You focus on the case and getting better," she told him. "We're a team. There are going to be times when you're going to have to do for me. That's marriage."

"I love you," he said, wishing he could hold her close for a little longer.

CHAPTER TEN

Friday

Hank figured Agatha was right—they'd most definitely outstayed their welcome at the Hill Country Resort.

It had been fine when things had been on an even keel —he and Agatha had caught the person responsible for killing off the hotel's celebrity chefs—and to show his thanks, the owner, Robert Swan, had given them a free wedding reception and a suite whenever they needed it.

The only problem was, Robert hadn't been counting on Hank's sisters showing up and staying two full weeks at the resort. There was nothing that could make up for that trauma. But now Hank was back, lying in bed in one of the plush suites on the morning of his wedding, waiting for a killer to come hunting for him.

No, he was pretty sure all of their access to the resort would be revoked after this stunt. He and Robert had become friends and had more in common than he'd thought when they'd first met, but who could blame him for wanting Hank and Agatha out of his life.

Retirement hadn't gone as he'd planned. He'd ended up

working as much as he had when he was on the force full time. He'd always loved his work, but there was a reason he'd retired. It was time. It was time to do other things and have other interests. He had a lot of life left to live. That's not to say he wouldn't still have his hand in law enforcement from time to time, but his priorities had changed. The thought of moving out to the country with Agatha and raising chickens and building a barndominium—whatever the heck that was—had become very appealing over the last few weeks.

He started his day off like every day since losing the use of his legs. He went through his exercises and assessed his moving, trying to detect any movement that hadn't been there the previous day. He hadn't lost hope—yet. Those moments when his legs had moved involuntarily made him think healing was just around the corner.

There was a knock at his door. "Hank, you up?" Agatha asked.

"Sure, come on in," he said.

She opened the long wall of curtains and let the sunlight come in, and he automatically threw a hand over his eyes.

"Sorry," she said, grinning. "It's a beautiful day to get married. And we have a lot of work to do so this scum doesn't ruin our wedding day."

Before they had called it a day the night before, they'd all hatched a plan for trapping the killer. Although Hank and Agatha would be safely tucked away and guarded at the resort, she'd texted Heather and told her since their home had been destroyed and someone was out to get them that they were hiding out at the Sunshine Motel off the highway and she told Heather she'd pick her up early so they could do all of the things women do on their wedding day.

Heather had no clue it was a ruse, and had texted endlessly about hair and makeup and manicures until Hank thought Agatha might kidnap him so they could run off and elope.

Agatha had also made it a point to tell Heather to make sure she kept their location a secret while the police were still looking for Killian Flynn. Heather was the worst secret keeper in the world, but that wasn't the point. As long as their calls and text messages were being intercepted by JT Intel, and Heather believed everything was happening as normal, Killian Flynn should show up to kill Hank at the Sunshine Motel right on schedule.

"You ready?" Hank asked.

"For the wedding?" she asked, her smile lighting up the room. "Never been more ready for anything in my life."

"Isn't it unlucky for the bride and groom to see each other before the wedding?" he asked.

She blew a raspberry. "Nonsense. We're too old and practical to believe in that drivel."

He had to laugh. "I adore you."

"Good thing," she said. "You haven't woken up next to me with morning breath and bed head. No take backs after tonight."

"I'll risk it," he said.

"They're putting me through the works down in the spa," she said. "I've got to be there soon. I'm kind of scared."

"You think Heather is going to be mad?"

"Nah, she'll be fine once Flynn is scooped up and she can join me here to get pampered. A massage goes a long way with Heather. Rodriguez is still assigned to me for the day. I think she likes this assignment."

Hank's lips twitched. "What's not to like? Though I can't picture Rodriguez getting her nails painted."

"I just hope Coil returns my Jeep in one piece," she said. "I know he said a woman pretending to be me was going to be driving it as a decoy, but—"

"You don't trust her to take care of your baby," he finished for her.

Now it was her turn to laugh. "It's silly to be that attached to a car."

"It'll be fine," he said. "Everything is going to go according to plan, and this will all be wrapped up by lunchtime."

"Have you checked the surveillance cameras in the motel room Coil set up?" she asked.

"Not yet, but I'm not going to miss the action. I can watch the whole thing from my phone. Ain't technology grand?"

"Only when it's not being used against you," she said. There was another knock at the door and Rodriguez announced her presence.

"That's my cue to go get beautiful," Agatha said.

"I don't know how it's possible for you to be more beautiful than you already are," he said, kissing her hand.

"I could get used to romantic Hank," she said cheekily and headed out to meet Rodriguez.

As soon as she left, Hank called Coil to make sure everything was set up and ready to go. Since his laptop was on the nightstand, he grabbed it and logged into the secured video network to monitor the action in room 113 at the Sunshine Motel.

"Y'all ready to lock and load?" Hank asked Coil when he came on the line.

"Always," Coil said. "I hope you're not worrying about us instead of focusing on marrying that pretty lady."

"Don't worry," Hank said. "I'm focused where I need to

be. I just want to make sure my best man stays safe. I think you've still got our wedding rings."

"Right here in my pocket, and don't you worry about a thing. I've got the best spec ops cops in the business waiting to take this scumbag down."

"I know you'll get him," Hank said. "I wish I could be there with you, but here is the next best thing. Let me know if you need me."

"10-4," Coil said and disconnected.

Hank made sure he had a good online connection and set up the laptop so he could monitor the motel while still taking notes for the investigative files. There was another knock on his door, and he blew out a breath of frustration. This place was like Grand Central Station.

Dr. Sullivan was supposed to check on Hank's progress this morning, but he still had time before his appointment, so he didn't know who could be at the door. He grabbed his gun from the nightstand and hid it under the covers.

"Hank, you decent?" Hazel called out. "We're coming in."

If he hadn't been decent he certainly wouldn't have had time to get that way. His sisters pushed their way into the room, making the oversized room feel impossibly small. They had a way of sucking the energy out of everything they surrounded, him included.

"It's your wedding day," Betty said excitedly.

"He don't look too happy about it to me," Gayle said. "Having cold feet?"

"Of course not," Hank said.

"Too bad," Gayle told him. "Girl's going to drive you to an early grave. First it's your legs, next it'll be your ticker and you'll keel over from a heart attack."

"Oh, stuff it, Gayle," Patsy said. "You're such a stick-in-the-mud. This is Hank's wedding day. He's decided to marry Agatha, and I think it's all time we just accept it."

"What are you looking at on your computer?" Brenda asked. "It's not one of those dirty movies, is it? I don't think your bride would appreciate that."

Hank felt the color rush to his cheeks, but Patsy saved him from having to answer.

"That's a surveillance camera," Patsy said, coming over to sit on the bed next to him. "There's an undercover op going on right under our noses, girls!"

Before he knew what was happening all five of them were piled on the bed next to him, oohing and ahhing over the potential of catching a killer.

"Quiet down," he said, noticing someone moving in the parking lot.

"Is that a cop?" Patsy asked, pointing to the figure.

Hank watched and shook his head. "That's not a cop."

The man had appeared out of nowhere, and the weapon at his side was barely visible in the shadows. But Hank saw the gun as the man crept along the first floor to room 113. He just hoped Coil could see him as well. He didn't open their comm line. The distraction could cost someone their life.

Then his phone buzzed and a text message came on the screen.

You see this? Coil asked.

Yes, Hank replied. *I've got a solid visual. That's Killian Flynn.*

Coil didn't respond, but Hank knew Coil was issuing orders to the cops working the op. Hank's gut clenched as he watched Flynn kick in the door of the room where he thought Hank was waiting—speed, surprise, and violence—just like when he'd broken into the house.

Hank's sisters pressed into him and he could sense the tension among them as they watched and reality began to sink in. He was lucky to be alive. They all were. Betty laid her hand over his and squeezed.

There was a dummy body in the bed, and gunfire erupted as Flynn unloaded his magazine into the bed. And then the monitor was filled with smoke and noise as a flash-bang was thrown through the door and cops rushed in with weapons drawn. All he could do was pray that no one got caught in the crossfire.

When the smoke cleared, Flynn was on his stomach, a cache of weapons on the floor beside him, and his hands and ankles were zip-tied.

"Wow," Hazel said.

"That man sure wanted to kill you dead," Patsy said, wiping beads of sweat off her upper lip.

"Looks like it," Hank said softly.

His cell phone buzzed and he hurriedly answered. "Coil," Hank said.

"We got him," he said.

"I saw. Good work. And let me tell you how glad I am to be here rather than in that motel."

"No kidding," Coil said. "You want to be here for the interrogation."

"More than I want to breathe," Hank said. He looked at his sisters as he talked to Coil. "Doc Sullivan is going to be here any minute to check me out, and then I'll get a ride into town."

His sisters perked up at that. Since Agatha had rented the van, they hadn't gotten to be his taxi like they'd planned.

"All we need him to do is flip on Jarvis Turner and we'll have this thing wrapped up before you need to be at the church," Coil said. "You going to need me to help you get into that tux?"

"Yep," Hank said. "And I could use a ride too."

"What else are best men for?" Coil asked. "See you in a few."

CHAPTER ELEVEN

Hank had interviewed thousands of criminals over the course of his career. Some of them had committed unspeakable acts against innocent people. He'd been shot, stabbed, punched, and kicked by criminals, and yet, he'd always managed to keep his emotions in check. Until now.

He wasn't sure why. Maybe it was because he had a future ahead of him for the first time in a long time. But he had to get himself under control. If Flynn saw his anger, he'd know he had power over Hank.

The interrogation room was small and dingy with old industrial gray carpet and walls that needed fresh paint. There was no one-way mirror like they showed on television, but there was a security camera in the corner so people in the other room had access to audio/visual.

Flynn was still decked out in his tactical gear—black BDUs and boots—and Hank knew the team had confiscated a whole arsenal off of him before they'd put him in cuffs. If Flynn had been better trained, there would have been a lot of lost lives that morning. As it was, Flynn was as incompetent as the other members of his team.

"So you're the last man standing," Hank said, looking him in the eye. "I have to say, when we first started this investigation we were a little worried. And then we realized you guys were probably the worst mercenaries in existence. Did you even pay attention while you were stationed at Ft. Hood? Your military files show failed or mediocre marks across the board. Is that how you've lived your whole life? As a failure?"

Flynn turned his head to stare at the wall, but Hank could see his jaw clenched in anger and the vein throbbing in his temple.

"Don't want to answer that, huh?" Hank asked. "No problem. You don't have to talk. Why don't you let me talk for a bit, and I bet by the time I get done you're going to be so ready to talk I won't be able to shut you up."

Hank paused for dramatic effect and then dropped a fat file folder on the table.

"Let me tell you a story about a man named Killian Flynn who will probably get the death penalty, but I personally think that's getting off too lightly. I'd much prefer seeing you rot away in a prison cell with no chance of parole.

"Five soldiers," Hank said, taking photographs from the folder. He pointed at the first picture. "Dustin Hobbs. Died last week at the meatpacking plant y'all were using for a home base. I know because I put a bullet in him." Hank laid two more photographs next to the first one. "Robby Bowers and Jack Hayes. Army buddies of yours. Also dead. Killed by one of my associates." Then he placed the photo of Ivan Marko. "And the last of your merry men. Ivan Marko. Croatian national who went AWOL when he fell in lust." Hank slammed another picture on the table of Lorelei Watson. "She's not dead. At least not yet. But old

Ivan was gunned down by an old lady in the middle of the highway."

Hank spread his hands wide. "Mediocre in life and death. Every one of them. Who do you think is going to take the fall now that your buddies are dead? Not Ms. Watson. Her brother can afford a whole platoon of attorneys, and we can't tie her to the murders anyway. But you, Flynn. We can tie you to everything. Someone has to take the fall for killing a cop. And then there's this."

Hank pulled out the crime scene photos of what was left of the medical examiner and his assistant and put them on the table. It was a grisly sight to see. Next to that he put the crime scene photos of Brad Hartley and Gloria Chimes. "Maybe you can place the blame of Brad's death on one of your pals. But not Gloria's. We know she was tied up with Brad and bad business over at the funeral home. But the fact is, all of your friends were dead when Gloria was killed. You know who that leaves?"

Hank waited for Flynn to respond, but he was silent. Though he did turn his gaze to the picture of Gloria Chimes.

"Someone beat her to death and then stabbed her with a pair of scissors," Hank said softly. "It wasn't a quick job. It took time to beat her like that. A lot of rage in her killing. Do you have that kind of rage in you, Flynn? Maybe you and Gloria were having an affair."

"I barely knew her," Flynn said. "You ain't pinning her murder on me. I never touched her."

"Who?" Hank asked. "Lorelei? It took a lot of strength to do that much damage to Gloria. Somebody about your size who is the only man still alive in this whole fiasco."

Flynn swallowed hard, and Hank pressed.

"It's okay," Hank said. "You don't have to say anything. We've got enough to charge you with murder and throw away the key. You know, this is Texas. I think you rotting in a cell for the rest of your life is what you deserve, but people around here are pretty fond of the death penalty."

He picked all the photographs up and put them back in the folder. "It's fine if you want to take the heat all by yourself."

Hank backed up from the table and rolled to the door, the file in his lap.

"Where are you going?" Flynn asked, licking his lips nervously.

"We've done our job. You're about to be processed and sent over to the jail. And as much as I'd like to see you in an orange jumpsuit, I'm a little busy tonight. I'm getting married."

"I told you I didn't kill that lady," Flynn said. "I want a deal. I can tell you who did it, but I want a deal. He's the one who should be in prison. We just worked for him, but all this was his idea."

"Who?" Hank asked, not bothering to move from his place in front of the door.

"I want a deal," Flynn said.

"We can work a deal," Hank said. "But that's not how this works. The DA is more than happy for you to be the scapegoat. You've got to give us something solid before we can start talking deals."

"Jarvis Turner," Flynn said.

"The computer guy?" Hank asked, pretending ignorance. "The one who owns the largest tech company in the state? You want me to believe he's behind this. I've seen him at parties with the last two presidents."

"That's the guy," Jarvis said, nodding. "Lorelei is his sister. Or half sister. Whatever. But I'm telling you he's the one who hired us. He pays us in cash to run bodies from Brad's funeral home to the border."

"Oh, yeah," Hank asked. "Did you know what was being transported in the bodies?" Hank could tell Flynn was gearing up to lie, so he sweetened the deal a little. "You realize the more truthful you are with us, the more lenient the DA is going to be."

"Sometimes it was guns, sometimes it was explosives," Flynn said, taking the bait. "Depended on the buyer."

"Who set up the buyers?"

"Jarvis did," Flynn said. "He's got all the international connections. He'd make the deal, Brad would come bag the bodies, and then the guys and I would transport."

"What about Lorelei and Gloria?" Hank asked.

Flynn shrugged. "They were just chicks. Marko and Lorelei hooked up while he was still at Ft. Hood. She's the one who kept talking about her big deal of a brother, and that she could set us up with jobs once we were discharged. And Gloria, well, at first I thought she just worked for Brad, but then we found out that she and Jarvis were a thing, and Jarvis was using her to keep tabs on Brad."

"Is that why Brad died?" Hank asked, the lightbulb starting to turn on.

"Brad found out Jarvis was using the funeral home to funnel the money through, and it ticked Brad off because he thought it was putting him at risk of getting caught. And then Brad figured if the extra money was being funneled through the funeral home, then he was entitled to a bigger piece of the pie."

"And Jarvis found out he was skimming and had y'all get rid of Brad," Hank said.

"I'm not confessing to no murders," Flynn said.

"You don't have to," Hank said. "You've already said you knew there were explosives in the body. That's what killed three people at the morgue, so that's on you. And since your buddies were preoccupied with dealing with Marko being shot and you weren't with them, then that leaves you as the one who took care of Brad. See how the puzzle pieces all fall in line when you tell the truth? The DA is really going to appreciate that."

"I was just doing my job," Flynn said. "The order came straight from Jarvis. I've got the whole thing on my phone. He's the one who should go to jail for murder. It was his idea. I told you I'd give you Jarvis, and that's what I've done. I don't want to go to jail."

"Seriously, Flynn?" Hank asked. "You're going to go to jail. There's no way you're getting off with everything you've done. I'm sure the DA would be glad to lessen the charges on the three deaths that happened due to the explosion. You could probably cop down to accessory if you play your cards right. You'd have a lesser sentence and be eligible for parole with good behavior."

Flynn nodded. "I want that. That sounds good."

"Well, then," Hank said, nodding, not bothering to mention that that they had him cold on Brad's murder, and that would be a whole separate charge. "Who killed Gloria?"

Flynn snorted, feeling much freer now that he thought he was home free. "Jarvis killed Gloria. They were a thing, but man, were they dysfunctional. She had that kid and swore it was Jarvis's, but he never believed her until she took him to court. He had to pay out the nose in that child support settlement. He was ticked. She was already working for Brad at that point, and I think he buttered her up and was stringing her along so she did what he wanted."

"Sounds like a real swell guy," Hank said.

"He's a scary dude," Flynn said. "Looks like a nerd, but his eyes—man, his eyes are pure evil."

"You've been a big help, Flynn," Hank said, trying not to let his disgust show. "Sheriff Coil is going to get in touch with the DA, so y'all can all have a chat about your future. Tell me one thing though, if you would."

Flynn grunted.

"How did you know I was in that hospital? They don't give out names, especially the names of cops."

"Jarvis sent me your name and picture and where you were, and he told me you were responsible for taking out my team. I told him I'd do the job for free. It was the least I could do."

Hank grunted. "Where's Jarvis now?"

"No idea," he said. "He's got a big place in a gated community in Austin, but we always met at his sister's place."

"The house she's renting from Dustin Hobbs's mom?"

Flynn looked surprised. "How'd you know about that place?"

"Sometimes cops just know things," Hank hedged.

"That's a drop house," Flynn said. "New assignments, cash, new identities, weapons. We put in an order for what's needed and it shows up at the house under the floorboards. But Lorelei lives in one of those big old houses with a pool over in Salado. I've only been there once, but I know Jarvis and his sister are close, so she'll know where he is."

Hank nodded and the door opened and Coil was standing there. "DA's on his way over," Coil said. "The ball is in their court. Let's go get you married."

"Those are the sweetest words I've ever heard," Hank said, feeling the weight lifted from his shoulders. Everything was wrapped in a nice neat bow. Someone else could bring in Lorelei and Jarvis and book them. He had a date he couldn't miss.

CHAPTER TWELVE

Agatha hadn't realized what her wedding day would mean to her. She'd waited a long time to walk down the aisle. In fact, she never thought she'd get married. Her career had always been her first priority.

But here she was, waiting for the doors to open so all eyes could be on her. Her dress was beautiful, her skin polished, and her hair carefully coiffed so her veil could be displayed.

What she hadn't expected was the overwhelming sadness that snuck up on her as she realized her father wasn't here to walk her down the aisle. In fact, the church was full of friends and Hank's family. She had no blood relatives left. At least none she knew about.

"Let's get this show on the road," Hazel said, clapping her hands. "No one can see these dresses we spent a fortune on unless we get to walk down the aisle."

The wedding planner smiled patiently and ushered Agatha out of the way so she couldn't be seen when the doors opened. Barbie Barnes had come highly recommended. She'd done all five of Heather's weddings, and

Heather swore by the woman. Said she was a miracle worker. Agatha had to agree. She'd left all the small details in Barbie's hands, and the church had turned out beautifully.

The music cued for the family to start making their way down to their seats, and Barbie opened the double doors that led into the sanctuary. "Nice and slow," Barbie reminded Hank's sisters. "One at a time."

"I remember, I remember," Hazel said, shoving Barbie aside and heading down the aisle like a racehorse at the Kentucky Derby."

Barbie sighed and brought Betty to the front of the line. It was clear Betty had been partaking of her daily gin and tonics, and her smile was dreamy as she floated haphazardly down the aisle.

"Next," Barbie said, a little less enthusiastic.

"That's me," Patsy said. "Who's that fine fella down front on Agatha's side? I'd like to take a bite of that."

"Who? Where?" Gayle said, pushing Patsy aside. "Oh, yes. I see. A little young for you, Patsy."

"Oh, but I'm sure he's just right for you?" Patsy asked.

"Well I do look twenty years younger than my age," Gayle said.

Brenda coughed behind Gayle. "Only because your second husband was a plastic surgeon."

Patsy snickered and went down the aisle to the front to sit with her sisters.

"I'm next," Brenda said, elbowing Gayle aside and marching like a general to the front.

Barbie looked like she needed a vacation, and her smile wasn't quite as bright as it had been when they'd first started.

Agatha was watching through a crack in the corner of

the door, and she didn't know whether to laugh or cry. At least Hank's sisters lived in another state. She was thankful for small favors.

"Your turn," Barbie said to Gayle.

Agatha watched as Gayle pasted on her beauty queen smile and strutted her stuff like she was on the Victoria's Secret catwalk.

"I've never seen hips move like that," Barbie said. "Seems unnatural."

"Honey, there ain't nothing natural about that woman," Heather said, slipping up behind Agatha.

"Where have you been?" Agatha asked. "I was starting to think you weren't going to make it."

Heather rolled her eyes. "I know my cues, honey. I've done this dozens of times. You've been out here pacing like a maniac, and I was taking a little catnap. If we're going to party hard tonight, we've got to be well rested."

"What's she doing?" Barbie asked.

They all stared as Gayle gave the handsome gentleman in the second row from the front a dazzling smile and then scooted in close beside him on the pew.

"Who is that man?" Heather asked. "He looks kind of familiar."

"You probably dated him if he's from around here," Coil said sarcastically. "But it looks like Gayle has called dibs for the night. Come on, let's get this show on the road."

"Heather, you're next," Barbie said, a little too brightly.

Heather shoved her bouquet at Coil and straightened her violet dress, adjusting her cleavage so she was on full display. "Thanks, sugar," she told Coil. "Weddings are great hunting grounds for the next Mr. Right."

Heather gave them a wink and then walked down the aisle to stand at the front of the sanctuary.

Agatha couldn't help but laugh. The giggles snuck up on her and she laughed until there were tears in her eyes.

"Stop, stop," Barbie said, making tissues appear seemingly out of nowhere. "You'll ruin your makeup."

By that time, Coil was laughing too. "Y'all should have eloped."

Agatha nodded. "Now you tell me."

Barbie hurriedly closed the sanctuary doors, and then fluttered around Agatha, straightening her train and veil.

"You ready to do this?" Coil asked. "You can always change your mind, you know."

"Hush," Agatha said. "I love that man. Let's go."

"Just what I wanted to hear," Coil said, slipping his arm in hers. "Thank you for giving me the honor of escorting you down the aisle. Your daddy would be proud of the husband you picked."

Agatha choked back a sob and waved her hand in front of her face so she wouldn't be a sobbing mess by the time she reached Hank.

"Ohmigoodness," Barbie said, using her tissues to fix Agatha's makeup at the last minute. "Stop all that sentimental nonsense. You can do that after the photographer goes home for the night. Now y'all take a deep breath. The music is about to start."

The organ sounded the first strains of the wedding march, and Barbie said, "Smile," just before she opened the double doors again. The church was full, and everyone stood to their feet, but Agatha didn't have eyes for anyone but Hank.

He sat in his wheelchair in front of the platform, looking dashing in his tuxedo, and his smile was as bright as the sun. She didn't notice Heather standing on the first step of the platform, or Pastor Sean with his Bible open behind

Hank. She didn't even realize when Coil started guiding her down the aisle.

All she knew was she was suddenly beside Hank and he was reaching for her hand. They could have been the only two people in the universe as far as she cared.

"You look beautiful," Hank said softly.

She smiled and squeezed Hank's hand and then looked back at Coil and said, "Thank you."

"Who gives this woman in matrimony?" Pastor Sean asked.

"I do," Coil said, his voice carrying through the sanctuary, and then he took his place behind Hank as the best man.

"Dearly beloved—" the pastor said, beginning the introduction of the ceremony. Agatha's mind was a blur. After the last couple of weeks she and Hank had, she wasn't sure if anything was even real. It was as if the pastor was speaking in water, and the words weren't quite penetrating. Then she started to panic because she wasn't sure when she was supposed to start saying her vows.

Hank leaned into her and whispered, "You okay?"

His question brought her back into focus, and she nodded at Hank and then looked apologetically at the pastor, but he was still reciting familiar words. "If anyone has objection to this marriage, speak now or forever hold your peace."

"I object," a man said from behind them.

Everyone moved as one and turned to face where the voice had come from, including Hank and Agatha.

"What in the world?" Agatha muttered, looking for the voice.

It was the man Gayle had decided to sink her claws into

and sit next to, and she started scooting away from him as if they weren't together.

Heather squeaked and pointed to the man. "I knew he looked familiar. That's Jarvis Turner."

"Down!" Hank yelled as Jarvis pulled a gun from beneath his jacket and pointed it straight at Agatha.

She froze, and the explosion of gunfire was deafening inside the church. She didn't know what happened. Something hit her from the side and sent her sprawling to the ground, and a heavy weight landed on top of her.

Everyone was in motion—people in their Sunday best crawling over and under pews—and then there was a mighty Tarzan roar and Hazel yelled, "Get him!"

Hank's sisters charged Jarvis Turner and tackled him to the ground. Patsy and Brenda sat on him and Betty kicked the gun out of his hand. Hazel pulled her .45 out of her handbag and cocked the trigger, so the sound resonated over the chaos around them.

Everything had happened so quickly, only a matter of seconds from the moment Jarvis had spoken to her lying on the floor. She looked over to see Hank's wheelchair toppled over, but Hank was nowhere in sight.

"Hank!" she yelled.

And then she rolled over and saw him lying on the ground, blood pooling beneath him.

"Oh, no. Hank," she said, crawling toward him.

Dr. Sullivan was there in the crowd, and she looked up for him, but he was already heading toward them.

"Are y'all trying to smother me?" Hank asked.

"Hank, are you okay?" Agatha asked. "Where are you hit?"

"It's just a flesh wound." And then Hank broke into raucous laughter.

"He's lost his mind," Agatha said to Dr. Sullivan. "Maybe he's lost too much blood."

"Hank," Dr. Sullivan said. "I'm going to roll you so I can see exactly where the bullet went in."

That only made Hank laugh harder. "I'm...I'm fine," he said.

"What in the world is so funny?" Agatha asked.

"I moved," he said, gasping for breath. "When I saw him point that gun at you, I just went into motion. I jumped out of that wheelchair and tackled you. I jumped. Do you know what that means?"

He didn't let her answer.

"It means my legs work." And then he started laughing again. "Look!"

Agatha watched as Hank wiggled his legs. "Great," Agatha said. "But you've been shot. Maybe we could focus on that first."

Dr. Sullivan pulled Hank's tuxedo jacket back and tugged his white dress shirt open, showing Hank's abs. If it weren't for the blood, Agatha would've taken a moment to appreciate all the working out he'd been doing lately.

"Looks like the bullet grazed your side," Dr. Sullivan said. "It's just a burn, and you're bleeding like a stuffed pig, but nothing a little gauze and bandage can't handle."

"We've got a medical kit in the back," Pastor Sean offered.

"Perfect," Dr. Sullivan replied. "I can have you patched up and good as new. I've got my medical bag right here. Never leave home without it. As far as your legs, I told you that there was no telling when you'd gain feeling again. I guess saving Agatha was enough motivation to get you going."

Hank tried to stand, but only managed to make it to his knees.

"Take it easy, Hank," Dr. Sullivan said. "It'll take a little rehab before you're running marathons."

"Good to know," Hank said. "Because I couldn't run marathons before the accident." Hank winced as Dr. Sullivan cleaned the wound and started patching him up.

"Very funny," Agatha said.

"I thought so," Hank told her, winking cheerfully.

Agatha looked over in time to see Coil cuffing Jarvis and passing him off to another officer. "I figured you'd show up after we arrested your sister," Coil said. "Made you mad, didn't it?"

"I want the credit for this bust," Patsy called out, as Jarvis was led away.

Dr. Sullivan helped Hank back into his wheelchair and Pastor Sean restored order.

"Y'all still want to go through with the ceremony?" Pastor Sean asked.

"You bet," Agatha said. "But not here."

"Umm, I'm confused," Pastor Sean said.

"Pastor," Hank said. "We love working crime scenes together, but we don't want to get married at one."

Pastor Sean smiled and said, "I completely understand."

"I always wanted to get married beneath the stars," Agatha said. "And there's a park right across the street." She turned and looked at Hank. "Does that work for you?"

"As long as we're man and wife in the next twenty minutes, I don't care if we get married in the bathroom."

Agatha snorted. "Then let's go. Clock's ticking."

"May I have your attention?" Pastor Sean's voice boomed over his wireless microphone. "If you'll all move across the street to the park we'll finish what we started.

Our bride and groom are very anxious to get married before there are any other interruptions."

The audience erupted in cheers as they filed out of the church from all directions. Agatha grabbed the handles of Hank's wheelchair and started pushing him.

"You don't have to do this," Hank said. "I don't want you to ruin your dress."

Agatha rolled her eyes. "It'll make our wedding pictures more interesting. You do realize you knocking me over today brings things full circle, don't you?"

"How's that?" Hank asked.

"The first day we met, you knocked me over by spraying me with your water hose," she said.

"Huh," he said. "I don't know how I could forget about that. I should probably make it up to you."

"You're going to let me push you over?" she asked cheekily.

It was dusk outside, and stars were beginning to twinkle in the sky, the moon round and bright.

"Why don't we work our way up to that?" Hank said. "I'm sure you'll have plenty of chances to push me over once we get married." Hank put the brakes on his wheelchair, and pushed himself up to a standing position. "In the meantime, maybe we could hold each other up."

Agatha beamed and wrapped her arm around his waist as they made their way to the park and their future.

"Always," she said. "Now let's go make an honest woman out of me. I've got a tattoo I'm dying to show you."

Liliana and I have loved sharing these stories in our Harley & Davidson Mystery Series with you.

While Agatha and Hank get adjusted to the married life, make sure you stay in touch by signing up for our emails as we get ready to announce a brand new series.

Thanks again and please be sure to leave a review where you bought each story and recommend the series to your friends.

Kindly,
Scott & Liliana

Enjoy this book? You can make a big difference

Reviews are so important in helping us get the word out about Harley and Davidson Mystery Series. If you've enjoyed this adventure Liliana & I would be so grateful if you would take a few minutes to leave a review (it can be as short as you like) on the book's buy page.

Thanks,
Scott & Liliana

ACKNOWLEDGMENTS

Always a very special Thank You to our cover design artist Dar Albert at Wicked Smart Designs. The Best. Editor. Ever. Imogen Howson, we appreciate dearly.

ALSO BY LILIANA HART & LOUIS SCOTT

ABOUT LILIANA HART

Liliana Hart is a New York Times, USAToday, and Publisher's Weekly bestselling author of more than sixty titles. After starting her first novel her freshman year of college, she immediately became addicted to writing and knew she'd found what she was meant to do with her life. She has no idea why she majored in music.

Since publishing in June 2011, Liliana has sold more than six-million books. All three of her series have made multiple appearances on the New York Times list.

Liliana can almost always be found at her computer writing, hauling five kids to various activities, or spending time with her husband. She calls Texas home.

If you enjoyed reading *this*, I would appreciate it if you would help others enjoy this book, too.

Lend it. This e-book is lending-enabled, so please, share it with a friend.

Recommend it. Please help other readers find this book by recommending it to friends, readers' groups and discussion boards.

Review it. Please tell other readers why you liked this book by reviewing. If you do write a review, please send me an email at lilianahartauthor@gmail.com, or visit me at http://www.lilianahart.com.

Connect with me online:
www.lilianahart.com
lilianahartauthor@gmail.com

f facebook.com/LilianaHart

instagram.com/LilianaHart

BB bookbub.com/authors/liliana-hart

ABOUT LOUIS SCOTT

Liliana's writing partner and husband, Scott blends over 25 years of heart-stopping policing Special Operations experience.

From deep in the heart of south Louisiana's Cajun Country, his action-packed writing style is seasoned by the Mardi Gras, hurricanes and crawfish étouffée.

Don't let the easy Creole smile fool you. The author served most of a highly decorated career in SOG buying dope, banging down doors, and busting bad guys.

Bringing characters to life based on those amazing experiences, Scott writes it like he lived it.

Lock and Load – Let's Roll.

Made in the USA
Middletown, DE
24 July 2021

44696222R00071